The Famous Five Adventures

WITH

GEORGE AND TIMMY

The Famous Five

Adventures with George and Timmy

Special thanks to Sue Welford and Dynamo Design

This edition first published in Great Britain in 2009
by Hodder Children's Books

A Catalogue record for this book is available
from the British Library

ISBN 978 0 340 99777 2

Printed and bound in Great Britain by
Clays Ltd St Ives plc, Bungay, Suffolk

The paper and board used in this paperback by Hodder Children's Books are natural recyclable products made from wood grown in sustainable forests. The manufacturing processes conform to the environmental regulations of the country of origin.

Hodder Children's Books
a division of Hachette Children's Books
338 Euston Road
London NW1 3BH
An Hachette UK Company
www.hachette.co.uk

See page 334 for individual copyright holder details.

Contents

This book is dedicated to Timmy, the best dog in the world. These stories are about the time before I first met my cousins, Julian, Dick and Anne. Timmy was just a puppy then, but he was already showing signs of the clever, loyal and brave dog he would grow up to be. He went on to become one of the most important members of the Five, joining in all our adventures and helping us to solve many mysteries.

George

Timmy, the Fearless Puppy

1

A new friend

'*Georgina*! What have you done?' cried George's mother, staring at her in horror.

'I've cut my hair,' said George, standing in front of the mirror in the kitchen. 'It was growing all around my neck and I hated it.'

'But you look just like a boy!' said her mother, gazing at George's short, dark curls then at the rest of her hair lying in a little heap on the floor.

'Good,' said George. 'That's exactly what I want to look like.' She threw down the scissors. 'I'm going to get on with building my tree-house now.'

'Boys' haircuts, tree-houses, whatever next!' George heard her poor mother sigh as she went out of the back door, slamming it shut behind her.

George went into the garden shed to fetch the hammer and nails and she was soon hammering and banging up in the tall old apple tree in the garden. In fact, George was making so much noise that it wasn't long at all before her father came charging out of his study.

'What is that dreadful noise?' he shouted with an angry look on his face. 'How on earth am I supposed to do any work with that racket going on?'

George's father was very tall, very dark and had an extraordinary-looking face with a wide forehead and fierce, dark brows. He frowned an awful lot, just like George.

'It's all right, Quentin,' said George's mother, trying to calm her husband down. 'It's only Georgina. She's building a tree-house.'

'Well, go and tell her to build it somewhere else,' said her husband. 'She's disturbing my studies. What's the point of living in a quiet house by the sea if people go hammering and banging all the time?'

George's father was a scientist. He spent hours in his study working out difficult scientific problems and became very bad-tempered when he was disturbed.

George and her mother and father lived in a large, three hundred-year-old, white-stone house on top of a small cliff overlooking the sea.

The house was called Kirrin Cottage even though it was too

big to really be a cottage. It had red roses growing round the old wooden front door and a garden full of flowers. The house had been in her mother's family for many years and she wouldn't dream of living anywhere else. George loved to sit upstairs in one of the rooms that overlooked the sea and dream of smugglers and storms and shipwrecks and all the exciting things that had happened years ago and might even happen again one day.

Below the cliff was Kirrin Bay. The bay was beautiful, with a wide sweep of yellow sand and a dear little rocky island guarding the entrance. On a small hill in the centre of Kirrin Island was a wonderful, mysterious ruined castle that had once stood proud and strong, looking out to sea. George's favourite thing in all the world was playing in the castle's two tumbledown towers or inside the ruined room across the stone courtyard where a huge old fireplace was built into one of the walls. She could get to the island by rowing her little wooden dinghy carefully through a reef of dangerous rocks, landing eventually on the golden sand of the little island cove. She loved the rabbits and sea birds that lived on the island and thought that the castle was the most eerie and exciting place she had ever seen in her life.

After her father's angry outburst about the terrible noise that George was making with her hammer, her mother gave a sigh and went outside to find her.

'Hello, Mummy,' said George, staring down from the tree with her brilliant blue eyes. She had nailed two planks together across the branches and was just about to nail another one to them. 'This is going to be such fun when I've finished it, don't you think?'

'I'm afraid you've got to come down, Georgina,' said her mother firmly. 'Father's busy and you're disturbing him.'

George jumped down from the tree with a big scowl on her face.

'Oh, Mummy, please don't call me Georgina. You know I hate it. Call me George.'

'Your name is Georgina,' insisted her mother. 'George is a boy's name.'

'I know,' said George, standing with her hands on her hips. 'That's why I like it. Most of all in the world I'd like to be a boy, so if you call me Georgina I shan't answer.'

'Oh, dear,' sighed her mother. 'Why can't you just be content to be a girl?'

'I don't know,' said George, screwing up her freckled nose. 'I just know that I hate doing things that girls do. Dressing in frilly frocks, playing with dolls and having pretend tea parties.' She pulled a face. 'Ugh, I hate them! I like climbing and swimming and running and sailing and I can do all those as good as any boy, so there.'

'And building tree-houses,' said her mother with a smile.

'Exactly,' said George, still scowling fiercely. 'Girls' games make me sick and I won't play them for anything.'

Her mother sighed again. 'Well, I wish you would make friends with some of the girls in Kirrin village. It would be lovely for you to have someone to play with. I thought about asking your cousins to stay for the holidays but Father said four children in the house would make too much noise.'

George's cousins lived in London. Their names were Julian, Dick and Anne but George had never met them. She didn't particularly want to, especially as one of them was a girl!

George scowled even harder at the thought of her cousins coming to stay at Kirrin Cottage. 'I don't want anyone to play with, Mummy,' she insisted. 'And I don't want any other children staying here. I like being on my own.'

'Oh, well, Georgina,' said her mother. 'It's up to you, I suppose. But you'll have to find something else to do for now, I'm afraid.'

Because her mother had called her 'Georgina', the little girl ignored her. She stood there with her hands in the pockets of her jeans, whistling and looking up at the sky in a very boyish fashion.

'Georgina, George. Did you hear what I said?' asked her mother in an exasperated voice.

'Yes,' said George. 'And I haven't any idea what I'm going to do now. I was having a lovely time and now Father has spoiled it.'

'You can finish your tree-house later when Father has finished his work,' said her mother.

'But Father has never finished work,' complained George. 'And even if he thinks he's finished then he quickly remembers he hasn't.'

George's mother sighed for the third time in a very short while.

George was right about her father. When he was busy, which was almost always, he even forgot what day it was, and if he didn't draw the study curtains back he wouldn't know whether it was morning, noon or night. He was so wrapped up in his work that he would often leap up in the middle of dinner to go and finish a problem they had thought he'd already solved. He spent hours in his study working on important scientific formulas and writing books about them. He often stayed there for days on end.

She patted George's short curls. 'Well, why don't you go up on the moor, darling?' she suggested. 'It's a lovely day, just right for a walk.'

'Oh, all right,' said George sulkily. She strode off through the gate at the end of the garden leaving her poor mother to put away the hammer and nails.

George climbed the steep path to the moor. She forgot that she was angry as she looked up at the vivid blue sky and the lazy cotton-wool clouds drifting by. She could hear a skylark singing in the distance and the smell of the heather blew towards her on the breeze. It was much too nice a day to be annoyed for very long! In fact, George was the kind of person who flared up easily but never stayed angry for long. She could be rude and haughty and very fierce at times but she was a very loving and loyal and extremely honest little girl.

George put her hands her pockets and strode along, whistling as well as any boy could. 'Girls' games,' she muttered to herself. 'I hate girls and I don't need anyone to play with. I'm all right as I am, thank you, Mummy dear!'

Soon, she was a long way away from Kirrin Cottage, high up on the moor with gorse and heather as far as she could see and the sound of the sea breaking against the base of the cliffs far below. She was all alone, just as she liked to be.

On that particular day, though, George was not going to be alone for very long. What she did not know was that very soon she was going to find a friend. Someone who would be the best friend anyone could ever have in the whole world. Even George!

2

A discovery

George was bowling along quite merrily when a most peculiar noise stopped her in her tracks. It was a whining, squeaking noise and it came from a clump of undergrowth by the side of the path.

She frowned. What on earth was it? Could it be a wild animal of some kind? A rabbit or a badger perhaps? George's curiosity got the better of her and she bent down to have a look.

'Oh!' exclaimed the little girl. There, sitting under a gorse bush, was a tiny puppy. George let out of a cry of astonishment and stretched out her hand. She grasped the puppy gently by the scruff of its neck and drew it towards her and up into her arms. 'Oh, you poor dear little thing!' she cried, holding the puppy against her and stroking its fluffy head. 'Where on earth did you come from?' She looked around but there was not a soul in sight. How on earth did the little creature come to be out on the moors, she wondered, all alone just like her?

George sat down with the puppy on her lap. He was a kind of sandy brown colour with scruffy fur and a very long tail. He had a little round black nose and huge, melting, brown eyes. As she stroked him, the puppy gave a little whine as if to say 'thank you for finding me' and licked her freckled nose and cheeks with his rough, pink tongue.

'Oh, you're so sweet,' said George. 'Where are your mummy and daddy?'

But there was no answer to her questions, only another little whine from the puppy. He snuggled down on her lap, happy not to be alone any longer.

George just did not know what to do. If she carried him back to Kirrin Cottage and the puppy's owners were somewhere around they would not be very pleased to return and find him gone. But then if they were around and they had left the puppy to play by himself then they did not deserve to have him. George suddenly began to feel very angry indeed. What kind of a horrid person would leave such a young animal all by itself?

Making up her mind what to do at last, George stood up with the puppy in her arms and began to walk all the way back home to Kirrin Cottage. She would ask her parents. They would know what to do!

After a little while, George's arms grew tired of carrying the puppy so she put him down on the path. He scampered along beside her, full of energy and so pleased to have been rescued by someone as nice and kind as this little girl. He had been very happy snuggled in her warm arms but now it was lovely to be springing along by her side.

The puppy gave little yapping sounds and ran after the sticks that George threw for him. Soon they were having a fine old game.

'Puppy! Puppy!' called George as the little dog ran off into the heather, then came bouncing back towards her. What fun he was to play with!

When she came to her gate, George picked the puppy up again and ran up the garden path and in through the back door. The woman who helped in the house was in the kitchen making some scones for tea.

'Joanna, look who I've found!' cried George as she hurtled in.

'Oh!' squealed Joanna as she saw what George carried in her arms. 'Where on earth did it come from?'

George explained that she had found the puppy on the moor.

'Goodness me,' said Joanna. 'Who would leave such a sweet little creature on its own so far from home?'

'I've no idea,' said George. 'Someone perfectly horrid obviously. Whoever it was, they deserve to be punished. It's a very cruel thing to do, don't you think, Joanna?'

'I certainly do,' said Joanna. She went to the fridge and took out a bottle of milk. She poured some into a saucer and put it on the floor. 'Here you are, Poppet,' she said to the puppy. 'Let's see if you're thirsty.'

'Do dogs drink milk?' asked George, who had never had a dog and did not really know anything about them.

'Yes, of course,' said Joanna. 'He's only a baby and all babies drink milk.'

They both watched as the puppy lapped hungrily.

'What kind of a dog do you think he is?' asked George.

'I've no idea,' answered Joanna. 'His head looks too big, his ears too pricked and his tail altogether too long. It's impossible to tell.'

'Well, I don't really care what kind of a dog he is,' remarked George. 'I think he's simply wonderful.'

'Who's wonderful?' asked her mother coming through the door.

'This puppy,' said George.

'Puppy!' exclaimed Mother. Then she saw what George meant. 'Oh, my goodness, Georgina. Whose is it?'

George was too thrilled about finding the puppy to notice her mother had called her Georgina. When her mother asked her who the puppy belonged to she wanted to say 'me' but she knew he wasn't really hers. Things didn't belong to you just because you had found them. She explained what had happened.

'Well, the best thing you can do,' said her mother, 'is to take him to the village and ask if anyone has lost a puppy. He may have wandered on to the moor all by himself.'

'All right, Mummy,' said George, pulling a sad little face. 'I suppose I'd better.'

When the puppy had finished his milk he ran over to George and growled and began to play with the laces of her plimsolls. George and her mother and Joanna thought that was very funny and all laughed loudly. So loudly, in fact, that Father came out of his study to see what the joke was all about.

'What's this!' he exclaimed when he saw the little dog.

'A puppy, Father,' said George.

'I can see that, Georgina,' said the tall man in a stern voice. 'I mean what is it doing here?'

Again, George did not protest about being called Georgina. She didn't want Father to be angry about her bringing the puppy home. She decided she had better keep in his good books. Sometimes George couldn't control her temper and would give hot answers to people without thinking. This time she just softly and sensibly explained all over again about finding the puppy.

To George's relief, her father was not angry at all. He bent and stroked the puppy. 'My word, he's a nice little fellow, isn't he?' he said as the puppy licked his hand. 'Someone will be very upset that they've lost him.'

'You'd better take him to the village now,' said Mother to George. 'You could try the police station too, to find out if anyone has reported a lost dog.'

'Very well,' sighed George. She picked the puppy up and went out feeling very sad. Having a dog would be such fun. In fact, it would be the best friend anyone could ever have. Wouldn't it be wonderful if no-one knew who he belonged to and she was allowed to keep him for ever.

To get from Kirrin Cottage to the village, George had to walk past the little harbour where the fishermen kept their boats. As she walked by, Alf, a fisherman's son, called out to her. He could see she was carrying a puppy and wondered if it belonged to her.

'Got a new puppy, George?' he called from where he was sitting on the edge of a boat mending a fishing net. He had met George several times before and knew she did not like being called by her proper name.

George walked down the steps towards him. 'I found him.'

'Found him?' cried Alf as he stroked the little dog and generally made a fuss of him. 'Where?'

Alf looked amazed when George told him. 'I suppose you don't know anyone who has lost a puppy, do you?' she asked, half-hoping he would say no.

Alf shook his head. 'No, no-one. It's very strange that he should be up on the moor all by himself, poor little tyke.' He stroked the puppy again. 'He's lovely.'

'Yes,' sighed George and went on her way.

The puppy struggled in her arms so she put him down and he trotted beside her, looking up at her now and then as if to make sure she was still there. He had been lost once and didn't want to get lost again. In fact, he felt so safe and secure with this little girl he would like to stay with her all the time from now on.

Just as George and the puppy were about to cross the sleepy high street a very large motorbike roared past.

'Careful!' cried George, scooping the puppy up into her arms as he very nearly stepped into its path. 'What horrid person is riding so fast through the village?' said George with a frown. Kirrin was usually very quiet with a general absence of noisy traffic and that was just the way George liked it.

'Wuff,' barked the puppy as if to say he didn't know, but he thought they were horrid too.

George crossed the street and went into the post office. The post office was part of the village store which sold everything from tintacks to tinned tomatoes.

The post mistress, Mrs Wood, was behind the counter. She was very short and rather plump and sat on a high stool. In fact, the stool was so high her feet dangled quite a long way from the floor.

Mrs Wood had a parrot in a cage hanging from the ceiling and it imitated the sound of the doorbell clanging as George and the puppy came through. Ding dong, ding dong! It was difficult to tell which was the real bell and which was the parrot.

'Who is it?' the parrot said as George went towards the counter. She chuckled. Mrs Wood's parrot always made her laugh. 'Who is it?' repeated the parrot loudly.

'Do be quiet, Polly,' said Mrs Wood. 'Can't you see it's the young lady from Kirrin Cottage?'

George winced. Being called a young lady was even worse than being called Georgina!

'Young lady,' said Polly. 'Young lady. Ding dong.'

George could not help grinning as she picked up the puppy to show Mrs Wood. 'You don't know who he belongs to, do you?' she asked.

'Oh, what a sweet little creature,' exclaimed Mrs Wood. 'Where did you find him?'

By the time George had walked all round the village it seemed she had explained a dozen or more times where she had found the puppy. But no-one had lost him. No-one knew where he came from. She stopped one or two people in the street and asked them but none of them knew anything about a puppy. A tall man wearing a dark leather jacket ignored her and pushed past rudely when she tried to approach him.

'Rude man!' George muttered as she made her way along to the police station to ask if anyone had reported a lost dog.

PC Moon looked over the counter at the puppy, then opened a big blue covered book he kept beside him. In the book he kept a note of things that had been lost and found.

After he had looked through several pages, the policeman shook his head. 'Sorry, Miss, no-one's reported a missing puppy.'

'Well, what should I do with him, then?' asked George, scowling a little because the policeman had called her 'miss'.

'Well,' said PC Moon. 'If no-one claims him within thirty days then you can keep him, if your parents agree.'

'Thirty days!' exclaimed George. 'That's ages and ages, the school holidays will almost be over by then.'

'Well,' said PC Moon. 'Those are the rules. Do you want me to phone the dog rescue centre? They'll keep him for that time if you like.'

George hugged the puppy close. She could not bear to think of letting him go. He snuggled against her and licked her hand as if to say 'please keep me for ever and ever'. Then George had an idea. She would ask her mother and father if she could keep the dog for the thirty days. She knew he would be much happier at Kirrin Cottage than at the dog rescue centre. He could help her finish the tree-house. She could take him for wonderful walks on the beach and row him over to the island, where they could play games in the castle. She could even take him to climb on the rocks where a giant shipwreck lay just below the surface of the water. The ship had once belonged to George's great-great-grandfather and had lain there for years and years. She knew the puppy would absolutely love it. The people at the rescue centre would be very kind to him but there would be lots of other dogs there and no-one would have the time to cuddle him or take him on adventures.

'I'll ask my parents if I can keep him for the time,' George said to the police officer. 'If they say yes I'll telephone you to let you know.'

'Right you are, Miss,' said PC Moon when he had written down all the details of where George had found the puppy and a description of what the little dog looked like. 'You give me a ring when you get home and let me know what your parents say. If they say yes and anyone comes in who's lost a puppy I'll send them over to Kirrin Cottage.'

'Thanks very much,' said George. She scooped the puppy up in her arms and went out.

On the way home she passed Alf again. 'Any luck?' he called.

She explained to him what the constable had said.

'What will happen if no-one claims him?' asked Alf.

'Well,' said George with a merry twinkle in her eye because she couldn't help feeling excited and thrilled at the thought of having a dog. 'I'm hoping that Mummy and Father will love him so much they'll want him to stay at Kirrin Cottage for ever!'

Alf grinned. 'Let's keep our fingers crossed then, shall we?'

'You bet,' called George as she waved goodbye to Alf and set off, whistling, towards home once more.

At Kirrin Cottage, George's mother was in the garden tending her flowers and vegetables. She listened carefully as George told her what had happened in the village. George put the puppy down and he scampered off towards the vegetable patch, poking his little black nose in between the rows of carrots and onions and beans as if he was exploring an exciting jungle.

'So, please, Mummy,' said George when she had finished explaining, 'please can we keep him here until someone claims him?'

Mother gazed at George, then at the puppy, who by now was quite happily chewing one of the beansticks.

George held her breath. Would Mummy say yes or no? If the answer was yes she would be the happiest, most contented little girl in the whole wide world!

3

A special meal

In the garden at Kirrin Cottage, George's mother was looking thoughtful. She wasn't at all sure it was a good idea for George to keep the puppy she had found on the moor.

'Please, Mummy,' said George once more. 'I know he'll be ever so good and I promise to keep him quiet when Father's working.'

Her mother sighed. 'Well, all I can do is ask your father,' she said, smiling suddenly. 'If he thinks it's a good idea then I do too.'

George was suddenly filled with happiness. She threw her arms round her mother's waist and gave her a big hug. 'Oh, thank you, Mummy! When will you ask him?'

'When he's in a good mood,' said her mother, hugging George back. 'You know there's always a right time and a wrong time with Father. You'll have to try to be patient.'

But being patient was not one of the things that George did best. She wanted to know if the puppy could stay at Kirrin Cottage until his owner was found. She could not possibly wait until Father was in a good mood to ask him. It could be ages and ages before that happened. In fact, he had been known to be in a bad mood for the whole of the school holidays with George not seeing him smile once.

Then she had a bright idea. 'If Joanna cooks him his favourite dinner that will make him in a good mood,' she said.

Her mother laughed. 'That's a very good idea, Georgina, er, George. Why don't you go and ask her?'

George skipped indoors with the puppy trotting beside her. He really was the sweetest little creature you could ever see. He was so keen on staying as close to the little girl as possible, it seemed as if he was attached to her feet by a piece of string.

As George opened the back door the puppy rushed in, slipping and sliding on the polished tiled floor of the hall and skidding into the kitchen. He came to a halt beside Joanna's feet just as she was trying to decide what to cook for dinner that evening.

'Are you still here?' said Joanna, bending to stroke the puppy. She looked up at George. 'You didn't manage to find out who owns him, then?'

George shook her head. 'No.' She went on to explain what PC Moon had told her about keeping the puppy for thirty days in case an owner showed up.

'And PC Moon said I could keep him here if Mummy and Father agreed and I do so want to,' she said breathlessly. 'And Mummy's going to ask Father so will you please cook his favourite dinner to put him in a good mood?'

Joanna smiled at the little girl's eager face with her dark curls bouncing above her vivid blue eyes. 'Well,' she said. 'Your mother bought some fresh salmon yesterday so we'll have that with new potatoes and salad. That's one of your father's favourite meals so I'll do that tonight, shall I?'

George grinned. 'Oh, yes please! And how about apple crumble and custard for pudding? You know he likes that too.'

'Very well,' said Joanna. 'But you'll have to go out into the orchard and pick me some cooking apples.'

'Oh, I will,' said George. She bent down and picked up the puppy. He had been growling and tearing at the rug in front of the stove, gripping the corner between his sharp little puppy teeth and shaking it to and fro. 'Do you hear that, Puppy? Salmon and new potatoes! If that doesn't put Father in a good temper then nothing will!'

The puppy looked at George with his little head cocked to one side. Then he stuck out his long pink tongue and licked her nose. Salmon and new potatoes sounded a very good idea indeed!

'I do believe that dog understands every word you're saying,' remarked Joanna as she went to the fridge to fetch the salmon.

'Of course he does,' said George. 'He's the most beautiful, clever dog in the whole, wide world!'

'I had a dog when I was your age,' said Joanna as she bustled about preparing the meal. 'Now he was the most lively and bright dog you could ever meet. He was wonderful and I loved him with all my heart.'

George sat on the floor playing with the puppy. He kept growling and pretending to bite her fingers. 'What was your dog's name?' she asked Joanna, looking up at her.

'Timothy,' said Joanna dreamily. 'He was brave and loyal and he went everywhere with me. People used to say he was like my little shadow.'

'Timothy,' murmured George thoughtfully. 'That's a jolly good name for a loyal and clever dog. I shall call this little dog Timothy too. It suits him very well, don't you think?'

'It certainly does,' said Joanna, gazing at the puppy with a smile on her round face.

George stood up. 'Right, that's decided, then. Come on, Timothy, let's go and pick some apples for Father's favourite pudding.'

Together, George and Timothy ran outside, down the garden and into the little orchard at the far end.

'Stay here,' she said to Timothy, pushing down gently on his back so he sat down by the tree-trunk. 'I shan't be a minute so don't try to follow me. Dogs can't climb trees, you know.'

Timothy watched as George climbed the tree as fast as a monkey. When he saw her balancing on a dangerous-looking branch he gave a worried yelp and tried to jump up the trunk after her, bouncing up and down like a yo-yo.

George looked down at him and giggled. She felt sure Timothy would have climbed up after her if he had been able.

She stuffed all her pockets full of apples and soon clambered down again.

'Good boy, Tim,' she said, bending down and giving him a cuddle before the two of them ran back indoors.

'Here you are, Joanna,' said George, tipping the shiny green apples from her pockets on to the table. 'Now we're going to find Father and tell him what's for dinner.'

Joanna picked up one of the apples and held it to her nose. 'Mmm, lovely,' she said. 'This apple smells of summer.'

George took one and sniffed it. 'So it does.' She put it to Timothy's nose so he could sniff it too.

'Wurf,' he said, making a sound in between a yap and a bark.

George and Joanna laughed.

'Now, I don't think you should bother your father for the moment,' the housekeeper said. 'He's very busy. Why don't you take Timmy out while I prepare these apples and get the rest of the meal ready. I'm sure the little fellow would love a walk.'

George suddenly remembered they didn't have any puppy food. What on earth was Timothy going to have for his dinner?

'Oh, dear. I don't know,' said Joanna when George asked her. 'You'd better go and ask your mother.'

So George ran back outside to find her. She was in the front garden now, tending the rambling rose that grew around the front door of the cottage. Timothy bounced beside George as she ran. He rather liked all this hurrying to and fro. It got rid of his puppy energy.

The first thing George told her mother was that she had decided on a name for the puppy.

'That's very nice,' said Mother. 'You can call him Timmy for short.' She was smiling but she also looked rather worried. 'You mustn't get too fond of him, dear. Supposing Father doesn't . . .'

But George didn't want to hear what would happen if her father wouldn't let Timothy stay at Kirrin Cottage for a while. She was very good at not listening to things she didn't want to hear so she just interrupted her mother and said, 'Please may I go to the village and buy some puppy food for Timmy? He's very hungry.'

'Yap, yap,' said Timothy, agreeing with her. He sat down on her left foot with his tail wagging nineteen to the dozen. 'Wurf, wurf,' he barked, trying to sound like a very hungry grown-up dog rather than a puppy.

George's mother could not help smiling. She reached into her coat pocket and took out her purse. She handed George a five-pound note. 'Take this to the pet shop and buy some puppy food. And you'd better hurry, they'll be closing soon.'

George's eyes shone. 'Thanks, Mummy.' She patted her leg. 'Come on, Timmy, good boy.'

The little dog followed George through the gate and on to the path that led to the village. He was so happy to be near her he trotted along beside her as good as gold. He had forgotten all about the loneliness and fear he had felt when he was up on the moor. Things were certainly looking up. He had a new name, a new mistress, and a lovely new house close to the sea. Life, Timothy decided, was very good indeed.

4

Father makes a decision

George and Timothy trotted along as if they had been friends for ever. George chatted away. Although she hadn't minded being alone before, she had to admit it was lovely to have someone to talk to. It was late afternoon and the sky had a rosy glow as the sun got ready to go down. Every now and then Timothy spotted something that caught his puppy attention.

Once, he dived into the hedgerow and came out with a stick. He laid it at George's feet.

'Timmy, you're so clever!' cried George, picking up the stick and throwing it. Timothy leapt after it, picked it up and trotted back to George.

George suddenly realized the shops really would be closing if they didn't hurry. She picked Timothy up, tucked him under her arm and hurried on towards the village.

At the little harbour she stopped and looked out over the sea. It was a warm, shimmering blue. Round the corner of the jutting cliff she could just see Kirrin Island and the ruined castle tower.

'See that, Timmy,' said George, holding the puppy up so he could get a better view, 'that island is going to belong to me one day. If Father lets you stay with me I'll take you there in my little boat. But you have to promise not to chase the rabbits or birds.'

Timothy looked up at her. 'Wuff,' he said solemnly, promising he would do no such thing.

George gave him a squeeze. 'We can have lots of adventures,' she said. 'It's the best place in the world.'

Timmy looked at the island with his little ears pricked up as high as they would go. It certainly did look a very exciting place indeed. He was not quite sure, though, that he liked the look of the great waves breaking against the rocks that seemed to go right round the island. They looked a bit dangerous to his puppy eyes!

By the time George and Timothy returned home, dinner was almost ready. As they came through the back door carrying a large bag of puppy food, Joanna was just dishing up the delicious-looking new potatoes.

'Please may we have a bowl for Timmy?' asked George as she dumped the bag of dog food on to the table. Timothy sat down at her feet staring hopefully up at the table. His little stomach had been rumbling for hours. He gave several little yaps and yelps and tried to jump up to grab the bag.

'Down, Timothy!' George commanded sternly. Straightaway Timothy sat down to wait patiently while she found a bowl and tipped some food into it. She placed it on the floor with a bowl of clean water beside it. Immediately the little dog dived towards the bowl, gobbling up the food as if it might disappear if he didn't.

'My goodness,' said Joanna. 'He's got an appetite!'

George watched as Timothy licked the last remnants of the food from the bowl. 'He was starving,' she said. 'Poor old Timmy.' She picked up the bag and tipped some more food into the bowl. Timothy gobbled that up too, then quickly lapped some water to wash it down.

George laughed when she saw he was so full of food his tummy had grown as round as a barrel. She bent down so the dog could lick her face and say thank you for his dinner. She picked him up and cuddled him close. 'Isn't he wonderful?' she said to Joanna.

Joanna stood looking down at the little girl and the dog. 'I hope your father lets him stay here,' she said. 'Otherwise I know someone who's going to have a broken heart.'

'What's this? Who's got a broken heart?' A deep voice came from the doorway and George's father stood there, frowning. 'I thought I could smell salmon and new potatoes,' he said. 'What are you doing rolling on the floor with that dog, Georgina? Why is he still here?'

George scowled when she heard her father call her Georgina. Then she managed to smile. If she complained about her name it would be bound to put Father in a bad mood, fresh salmon or no fresh salmon.

She quickly explained about asking everyone in the village if they knew who Timothy belonged to and then what PC Moon had said.

'Thirty days!' said George's father, still frowning. 'So where is he going to live in the meantime?'

'We were going to ask you if he could stay here, Quentin,' said his wife from the doorway. She had been upstairs getting changed for dinner and had heard Father and George talking in the kitchen.

'Here!' George's father frowned. 'But what about my work?'

'He'll be ever so good,' said George. 'And I'll keep him quiet, honestly I will.'

'Yap,' said Timothy as if to say, yes, he would be quiet as a mouse when Father was working on one of his important scientific projects in his study.

George's father stared down at the little dog. Timothy was sitting under the table, staring out at him from under his shaggy eyebrows. His tail wagged uncertainly, thump, thump on the floor. He knew that George loved him dearly and that her mother and

Joanna thought he was sweet too. But he wasn't at all sure about this towering, dark man who frowned down at him from such a long way above his head. Maybe he should try to make friends with him? After all, he was the little girl's father, so he couldn't be that fearsome, could he?

George's father was just about to speak again when Timothy came out from underneath the table and sat by his feet. Then, tired from all the games he had played with George and from the two long walks to the village, and such a huge dinner, the puppy lay down with his head resting on the toe of Father's shiny, brown shoe. He gave a deep, deep sigh, closed his eyes and suddenly fell fast asleep.

George's father did not move. He stood there looking down at Timothy.

'There,' said George. 'He likes you. Now you've got to let him stay. After all, Father, we have got salmon and new potatoes today and apple crumble for pudding.'

'Apple crumble? Mmm!' said George's father, gently removing Timothy's head from his shoe. He went to take a peep in the oven. 'My, my, that does look good, Joanna.'

'Father!' exclaimed George, forgetting to be patient. 'What about Timmy?'

'Timmy?' frowned her father. 'Who's Timmy?'

'The puppy, Quentin, dear,' said his wife patiently. 'George wants to know if we can keep him here until he's claimed.'

George's father frowned and sighed and shook his head impatiently. 'Oh, very well,' he said. 'But if he's a nuisance he goes to the dog rescue home. All right, Georgina?'

'George,' said George, forgetting to say thank you. 'I'm George and he's Timmy.'

'George and Timmy,' laughed her mother. 'The finest pair of scallywags you could ever meet.'

George crouched down and swept the snoozing puppy up into her arms. 'Hear that, Timmy? A fine pair of scallywags!'

The puppy woke up, yawned, then gave her nose a lick. George gave him the tightest hug she had ever given him. Then she looked up at her father with shining eyes. 'Thanks, Father. You've made me so happy!' Then she whispered in Timothy's ear. 'Just you wait, Timmy, you and I are going to have the best scallywag adventures in the whole wide world!'

5

George is defiant

'Timmy's going to sit under my chair while we have dinner,' said George as she helped Joanna lay the table in the dining-room.

'Oh no he isn't,' said her father sternly, coming in and sitting in his chair at the head of the table. He spread a snowy white napkin on his lap. 'Dogs don't belong in dining-rooms.'

'But where will he go?' asked George in a worried voice.

'He'll have to stay in the kitchen,' said her father firmly.

'But he'll wonder where I am,' protested George, scooping the puppy up into her arms. 'He'll think I've deserted him like those horrible people who left him on the moor.'

'They might not have done it on purpose,' her mother reminded her as she came and took her place at the table. 'He might have wandered off and got lost all by himself. Now do as you're told, George, and put Timmy in the kitchen while we eat.'

'I want him to stay with me,' insisted George stubbornly,

standing in the doorway with a fierce frown on her face.

'NOT while we're eating,' said her father, refusing to budge. Once he made up his mind about something, nothing would change it. Exactly like George. 'Tell her will you, Fanny,' he added, looking at George's mother. 'She seems to go deaf when I speak to her.'

'No, I don't,' protested George. She put the puppy down on the floor and stood with her hands on her hips defiantly. 'And if Timmy is to stay in the kitchen I'll have my dinner in there too.'

Her father was getting red in the face with anger. His dark eyebrows knitted in a knot over the top of his nose. When he looked like that, fierce and stubborn, he very much resembled George. 'Georgina!' he shouted. 'You really are the most difficult child. Don't argue any more or you'll go to bed without any dinner at all!'

Although George's stomach was rumbling with hunger she felt she would much rather go without food than be parted from her new friend. As usual, though, Mother intervened to pour oil on troubled waters. She picked Timothy up and handed him to Joanna. 'I'm sure you can find Timmy a nice beef bone to chew on while we're eating,' she said in a soothing voice.

'I've got just the thing,' said Joanna, taking the puppy from Mother's hands.

'George, sit down and do as Father says,' insisted her mother. 'Timmy will enjoy having a bone on the kitchen floor, he'd only make a mess on the carpet in here.'

George sighed. 'Oh, all right, then,' she agreed reluctantly, not wanting Timothy to miss a treat. She pulled out her dining-chair with a sulky look on her face, plonked down on it and dragged it back closer to the table. She sat there as stiff as a ramrod, glaring at her father across the table. That's always the trouble with grown-ups, she thought angrily. They spoil everything!

Once Joanna had settled Timothy in the kitchen, she returned with the salmon on a long, fish-shaped plate. There was a dish of luscious steaming new potatoes sprinkled with parsley and a lovely fresh salad with crisp lettuce and radishes from the garden.

Mother brought in the mayonnaise and sighed as she sat down. By the look on her face George could tell she was thinking that keeping Timothy at Kirrin Cottage for a month would mean more battles than ever between her husband and her daughter.

George finished her meal in record time. 'Please may I get down?' she asked stiffly the very minute she had finished her pudding.

'Yes, of course, dear,' said her mother. 'You'd better go and see how Timmy is getting on with his bone.'

In the kitchen, the puppy was gnawing at a big beef bone

underneath the table. George went and sat cross-legged on the floor, watching him. He really was the dearest puppy she had ever seen. She was so lucky to have found him. Then her heart turned over. She loved him so much already that she knew she would love him even more by the time his month at Kirrin Cottage was over.

Secretly she hoped that no-one would ever come to claim him. Then she had a very good idea indeed. If she was very, very good during the time Timothy was here, and she trained him to be a well-behaved puppy then Mummy and Father might let him stay for ever.

The little girl made up her mind there and then. She would not have any more battles with Father. She would be as good as gold and do exactly as she was told. She knew it was going to be difficult being good for a whole month but somehow or other she really would try to do it.

While her mother and Joanna cleared away the dishes and washed them up, George took Timothy out to play in the garden. She was determined to begin his training straightaway.

First of all she taught him to sit down on command. She had found some crumbled-up pieces of biscuit in her pocket amongst the other things in there. Bits of string, her penknife, an interesting pebble she had found on the beach and some chewing gum wrappers. Every time the puppy sat down she told him he was a good boy and gave him a tiny titbit. The little dog was bright as a button and soon learned exactly what to do.

Then George walked round the garden commanding Timothy to stay at her heel. The puppy was not very good at this and he kept running off to chase leaves that were blowing around in the breeze. Eventually he sat down right smack bang in the middle of one of her mother's flower-beds and gave a huge yawn. He lay down with his nose between his paws and his big brown eyes began to droop. He gave a little sigh and fell straightaway into a doze.

George went to haul the puppy out, hoping that Mummy wouldn't notice some of her flowers had got bent and broken. She tried to straighten them but they kept flopping back over.

'You mustn't tread on the flowers,' she said sternly to Timothy even though he was too sleepy to listen.

Soon it was time for George to go to bed too and her mother came out of the back door calling for her to come in. The little girl picked up the snoozing puppy and carried him gently indoors.

Her mother stroked his soft head. 'He's a very sleepy baby,' she said. 'I've asked Joanna to look in the airing cupboard for an old blanket so he can lay by the stove tonight.'

George looked at her mother in horror. She had already made

up her mind that Timothy would sleep at the end of her own bed. She knew he would love her little bedroom with its sloping ceilings and wonderful views of the moor at the back, and side window overlooking the sea. She was going to show him her bookcase full of boys' adventure stories and books on sailing and fishing. 'He's going to sleep with me,' she said. 'He'll be awfully lonely down here.'

'Oh no,' said her mother firmly. 'I definitely won't allow dogs on the beds. Your father would have a fit.'

'But he won't hurt!' cried George. Her heart had sunk right to her toes at the thought of being parted from Timothy again.

Mother shook her head. 'No, George. Dogs have their place and it isn't in dining-rooms or bedrooms.'

'But, Mummy . . .' began George. Then she remembered her vow to be well-behaved and bit her lip. She gave a big sigh. Keeping her temper was going to be much more difficult than she had imagined. 'Well,' she said sulkily. 'If he cries all night, Mummy, it will be your fault.'

Joanna came into the kitchen with an old pink blanket in her arms. It looked soft and cuddly and George knew Timothy would be warm and cosy by the stove. She took it from Joanna as the housekeeper went to fetch her coat ready to go home.

George laid the blanket by the stove and patted it. 'Come on, Timmy,' she said, biting back tears of disappointment. George almost never cried. She thought it was a soft and babyish thing to do but this time she nearly couldn't help it. She had been so looking forward to having Timothy in her bedroom. She hated dolls and teddy bears and never took anything to bed with her other than her torch and a book and sometimes a length of string to practise fishing knots with. It would be so lovely to have Timothy there.

Timothy gave a little whine and looked up at her. His big brown eyes seemed to be pleading with her to let him come up to her room. She crouched down and stroked him gently. 'I'm sorry, Timmy, but Mummy says you have to stay here in the kitchen.'

The puppy gave another little whine. He understood every word his new mistress was saying. He had tried so hard to please her and now she was banishing him to the kitchen to stay there in the dark all alone for the whole night. He put his head on one side and softly licked her hand.

George gazed up at her mother, hardly able to stop the tears trickling down her face. She tossed back her dark curls. 'Please, Mummy . . .?'

But her mother was determined. 'I'm sorry, Georgina, if he comes to your room Father will be furious.'

George gave a little snort. Father would be furious! Now she was furious. Her mother had called her Georgina again just to make matters worse. Everyone was being so unfair. She put the puppy firmly on the blanket and waggled her finger at him. 'Stay!' she commanded, her voice cracking with fury and sadness. Then she looked at her mother, her brilliant blue eyes sparkling with tears. 'I won't be able to sleep you know, Mummy. And neither will Timmy. We shall both be tired out and very grumpy tomorrow.' She stamped out of the room and slammed the door behind her.

George stomped all the way up the winding, narrow staircase to her little room right up in the roof of Kirrin Cottage. She stormed over to the window and gazed out at the darkening sky. She could see the last of the sunshine rippling on the little waves that broke over the shore and in the distance the island castle looked dark and mysterious against the orange sky. She sighed and brushed away an impatient tear.

She had already broken her promise to herself not to cause any more battles. She was used to arguing with her father but hated to disagree with her mother, who was always so kind and gentle. She wanted to run back downstairs and cuddle her and say she was sorry but she was far too obstinate to do that. She just had to stew in her own juice.

George stripped off her jeans and shirt and put on her striped pyjamas. She crawled in under the bedcovers and lay looking up at the ceiling. She imagined Timothy all alone in the kitchen. He would be scared all by himself. He would be thinking he was lost on the moor again.

George sighed and tossed and turned for what seemed like hours. The house was silent and all she could hear was the distant hoot of an owl and the murmuring song of the sea. Then suddenly the silence was broken by a high-pitched bark and a whine that turned into a howl. Downstairs, Timothy had woken up from a restless doze and wondered where he was. Everything was dark and silent. Where was the little girl who had been so kind to him? Where was the lady who had given him that great big bone?

The puppy gave another sad little whine. He crawled across to the rug and began chewing the corner. Crunch, crunch went his little sharp teeth. He felt better with something to chew on. The rug tasted bitter so he spat out the little ragged bits of wool that had come off in his mouth. He got up and bumbled around in the dark for a while, bumping into the table leg and the chair in front of the window. He felt sad and lost and alone. Then he had an idea. Maybe if he barked again really loudly George would hear and come to rescue him.

Upstairs, George heard Timothy barking and whining. Suddenly she could not bear it any more. She grabbed her torch, flung back the covers and ran on tiptoes to her bedroom door. She threw the door open and listened. There was no sound from her parents' room.

George ran lightly down the stairs, the torch flashing a beam in front of her. There was a light under Father's study door. Her heart turned over. Father was working on some very important experiment and if the puppy disturbed him he might send him away and she would never see him again. She crept past as quietly as a mouse.

In the kitchen, Timothy was sitting under the table chewing the corner of the rug in between howls and barks. George bent to scoop him into her arms. 'Oh, Timmy, darling, don't worry,' she whispered. 'You can come to my room but you must be very, very quiet.'

The puppy was so overjoyed to see her his tail wagged until it was just a blur. George giggled as he licked her face all over and squirmed with happiness. 'Ssh!' she hissed. 'Now keep quiet!'

Then George noticed the ragged end of the rug and bits of wool all over the place.

'Oh, blow!' she exclaimed in a whisper. 'Now, we are in trouble.' She put Timothy down and he ran round and round, his tail still wagging. Then he crouched down and fixed his tiny sharp teeth on the end of George's trouser leg. He growled and shook it as if it was a rat.

'Timmy!' giggled George. 'For goodness' sake! This isn't the time to be playing games.'

She managed to prise Timothy's teeth away from her pyjama leg and gazed at the ragged rug. What on earth was she going to do? At last she decided to turn it round so the corner was underneath the table. Hopefully no-one would notice.

After that she quickly swept up the pieces of wool and tipped them into the bin. 'Come on, rascal,' she said to Timothy when everything looked ship-shape again. 'Up to bed, now.'

They were half-way up the stairs when her father's study door opened and the light went on. George quickly clicked off her torch and shrank back against the stairwell. She could hear Father muttering to himself as he made his way past her and along to the bathroom. George put her hand over the puppy's muzzle to stop him making a noise. Her heart was beating so loudly it seemed to echo round the walls and she was afraid Father might hear it and discover her hiding place.

It seemed hours before George's father came out of the bathroom and made his way to his bedroom although it could only have been a matter of minutes. Timothy was as good as gold. Something told him that if he made a noise it could be the end of his stay at Kirrin Cottage.

At last, Father's door closed and the coast was clear. Without

daring to switch on her torch George ran the rest of the way up the staircase and into her room. She plonked Timothy on her bed and lay down beside him, giggling when he licked her face. 'Now, Timothy,' she said sternly, 'you be as quiet as a mouse and I'll take you back downstairs before Mummy and Father get up. With a bit of luck, no-one will ever know you've been here!'

George lay down and pulled the covers over her. Timothy turned round and round, making a little blanket nest next to her. This was doggie heaven. A soft warm quilt and the person he loved most in the world beside him. He wished he could stay here for ever.

6

A surprising headline

In the morning, Timothy awoke first. He had spent a very quiet and comfortable night curled up on George's bed. He had not even had any nightmares about being lost on a cold and windy moor. He sat up, stretched and yawned, then clambered up to the pillows and began licking George's face. The sooner his mistress awoke, the sooner they could start having fun.

George flung her arm up to her face and opened her eyes. She had been dreaming of all the adventures she and Timothy were going to have.

'Hello, Timmy!' she cried, giving the puppy a big hug. 'Did you sleep well?'

'Wurf,' said Timothy, licking her again.

George remembered he was not supposed to be in her bedroom but down in the kitchen beside the stove. She quickly glanced at her bedside clock. It was half past six and no-one else was stirring.

The sun was shining through her window and she could hear the cry of the seagulls and the chug of fishing boats as they left the little harbour and sailed out to sea. If she hurried, she could get dressed and take Timothy downstairs before anyone else woke up.

In no time at all, the little girl had flung on her jeans and a jumper and was creeping down to the kitchen. She opened the back door and the puppy ran outside, jumping and hopping, pleased to be out in the fresh air on such a lovely morning.

The paper boy was coming down the lane on his bicycle. George went to the gate to collect the newspaper.

'Is that your puppy?' asked the boy when he spotted Timothy running up and down the flower-beds and in and out of George's mother's shrubs.

'Well . . . sort of,' said George, explaining that she had found him and that he was staying at Kirrin Cottage for a while.

'Lucky you,' said the boy as he pedalled off. 'I've always wanted a dog.'

'Yes,' called George. 'So have I.' And now I've got one, she added to herself.

George decided to take Timothy for a walk before breakfast. She went out of the back gate and along the easy path that led down to Kirrin Bay.

Timothy raced on ahead, his little legs going as fast as they could, his shaggy tail waving like a banner. Every now and then he turned round to make sure George was still following. They walked down the cliff path to the beach. Timothy ran to the water's edge and began barking at the waves as they broke and crunched on the shore. When the water ran back he dashed after it, then turned and fled as a new wave broke and chased him up the beach.

George laughed to see the little dog having such a lovely time.

They walked along the shore for a little way then George's tummy began to rumble. She decided it was time to go back home for breakfast. Timothy was having such a good time he didn't want to leave. He had found a piece of driftwood and was attacking it, growling and shaking his head like a fierce grown-up dog.

'Come on, Timmy! Heel!' George called but the little dog ignored her. She decided that if she began to walk back he would follow. She strode off back towards the cliff path and as she turned to see if he was coming she thought she saw someone at the far end of the beach. A strange, dark figure with what looked like a very large head was disappearing rapidly round the rocky headland. She frowned. It was very early for someone to be walking along the beach. Who on earth could it be? She hated the thought of anyone else being on her little piece of seashore. She liked to think it belonged to her and no-one else. There were a few holidaymakers in Kirrin at this time of year but they didn't normally come to

Kirrin Bay. George usually had it all to herself, which was just the way she liked it. Maybe it was a fisherman looking for some lost tackle? Or a hiker who had missed the footpath? It seemed very strange that anyone should disappear round the headland. It didn't go anywhere and if you weren't careful you could get cut off by the tide.

But George forgot all about the mysterious figure as Timothy came bounding towards her with the driftwood in his mouth. 'Come on, good boy. We'll come back later,' she said as he reached her. 'You must be starving too and you can't eat driftwood for breakfast!'

By the time the two got back to Kirrin Cottage, Joanna had arrived and was cooking breakfast.

'My, you two are up early,' she said as they hurtled in through the back door. 'Has the little chap had his breakfast?'

'Not yet,' said George, fetching Timothy's bowl and filling it with dog food. 'We're both starving. What's for my breakfast, Joanna?'

'The usual,' said the housekeeper. 'Bacon, egg, fried bread and tomato.'

'Ummm, lovely,' said George, her mouth watering. She watched Timothy gobbling up his food, then lapping up the saucer of milk Joanna put down for him.

'Was he good during the night?' the housekeeper asked.

'Oh, yes,' said George with a grin. 'Weren't you, Timmy?'

'Wurf,' said Timothy, licking the last of the milk from round his mouth.

George's father came into the kitchen and picked up the newspaper that George had placed on the kitchen table. He went out without speaking. He had forgotten all about Timothy and had not even noticed George and Joanna standing there.

'I can see your father's in the middle of some very important work,' said Joanna with a knowing smile at her employer's absent-mindedness. 'You'd better keep that puppy out of mischief.'

George bent to pick the dog up. 'Oh, I will,' she said. 'I promise.'

When breakfast was ready, George left Timothy in the kitchen. She didn't want to risk any arguments with Father. 'Now don't you start on that rug again,' she whispered, giving the puppy what was left of yesterday's bone. 'Just make do with this for now. After breakfast we'll go and find you some things to play with on the beach.' She gave him a quick hug and went to sit with her mother and father in the breakfast room. Soon Joanna arrived with a big mound of crispy bacon, fried bread, fried eggs and tomatoes all in one warm dish which she placed in the centre of the table.

'Thank you, Joanna,' said George's mother and began serving some on to her husband's plate. He was too absorbed in reading the paper to notice the smell of the delicious food in front of him.

'Breakfast, Quentin!' said his wife in a loud voice.

'Thank you,' mumbled her husband from behind the newspaper.

'Timmy was good last night, wasn't he?' said George's mother. 'I slept like a log and didn't hear a sound.'

'Yes, he was good,' said George, giving a secret sigh of relief. She never told lies and she knew that if her mother had asked any questions about Timothy's whereabouts she would have had to answer them honestly.

'My goodness,' exclaimed her father suddenly. 'Listen to this.' He read out loud from the paper. 'Raid at Kirrin Village Post Office.'

There on the front page was a photograph of the village shop with Mrs Wood standing outside looking very upset.

'A robbery!' George said excitedly. 'What a thrilling thing to happen in sleepy old Kirrin!'

'It's not thrilling at all, Georgina,' said Father irritably. 'It's terrible. The thieves got away with thousands of pounds.'

George pulled a face. Her father had forgotten again that she would only answer to George. He really was quite impossible. She did not reply and turned her head away to look out of the window whistling a little impatient tune under her breath.

'Thousands!' exclaimed George's mother. 'I didn't realize Mrs Wood kept so much money on the premises.'

'Well, she did,' said her husband, continuing with the story. 'The postmistress was in her back sitting-room when a raider burst in,' he read. 'Mrs Wood was held hostage while the place was turned upside down.'

'Oh dear, poor woman!' exclaimed his wife. 'What a dreadful thing to happen!'

'I bet she was scared,' said George, trying to imagine what it would be like to be held hostage. She felt sure that if anyone tried to hold her hostage she would kick and scream until they simply had to let her go.

'Yes, I'm sure she was,' said her mother.

'The thief's motorbike was found crashed in the ditch on the coast road just outside the village,' George's father read on. 'But there was no sign of the robber. He and the cash box have completely disappeared.'

'How exciting!' said George, rubbing her hands together.

'Not exciting, just terrible,' said her father, suddenly folding up the newspaper. 'I don't know what the world is coming to if thieves and villains have to come to a place like this to do their dirty work,' he said, tucking the paper under his arm and standing up. 'Well,' he muttered. 'Better get on.' He turned and disappeared.

'Quentin, you haven't eaten your breakfast!' called his wife. But it was too late. He was already striding towards his study. Then the door banged and there was silence. That would be the last anyone would see of him until lunch-time and maybe not even then. They would just have to read the rest of the story about the Kirrin robbery some other time!

7

An exciting find

'What are you going to do with yourself this morning?' George's mother asked her as they helped Joanna clear away the breakfast things.

'I'm playing with Timmy,' said George.

'It's so good for you to have a companion,' said her mother, smiling. 'Although I would much rather it was one of the village girls and not a dog.'

'What's wrong with having a dog as a friend?' asked George, glaring. She hated always being told what was good for her. Children always knew what was good for them and they did not need grown-ups to tell them.

Her poor mother gave a sigh. 'Nothing, dear, it's just not quite the same, is it?'

'No,' said George fiercely. 'If you want to know, Mummy, it's much better!'

'Very well, dear, if you say so,' her mother said, sighing again. 'And Timmy is very sweet. Now run along and play, there's a good girl.'

George took a deep breath. She had promised herself she would not argue with her parents, but being called a good girl was almost too much to bear. She called Timothy and stormed off outside.

In the garden, George showed the puppy her tree-house. It was three planks nailed to a broad branch of the tree. Joanna's husband, William, who sometimes helped Mummy in the garden, had promised to bring George a big wooden box to serve as the living quarters.

'I'm not sure how we're going to get it up there,' said George to Timothy as they both gazed up at the tree. 'But somehow we'll find a way.'

Timothy gave a little bark and ran to the gate then back again. Right at that moment he did not really care about the tree-house. All he wanted was to get back to the bit of driftwood he had reluctantly left behind on the beach earlier that morning.

It was very warm on the beach now the sun was higher. Above George's head, seagulls whirled and dived in the clear blue sky and the sea was so calm there were hardly any waves to break on the shore.

George hummed a little tune to herself as she strode down the narrow path that led to the shore. She was so warm she took off her jumper and tied it round her waist.

Timothy scampered on ahead, his nose close to the ground as he searched for his favourite stick of wood.

He soon found it and came running back to George with it in his mouth. He growled and shook his head as she tried to take it from him.

'Leave, Timothy!' commanded George, trying to sound stern but all the time giggling because Timothy was so lovely and so funny.

At last, the little dog allowed George to take the stick and she threw it a long way down the beach for him to chase after. Suddenly a flock of seagulls flew in and landed a little way in front of him. He skidded to a halt, his ears pricked in surprise. Birds! What fun! He barked and ran towards them as fast as his legs would carry him. They flew off, squawking.

'Timothy!' called George at the top of her voice. 'You're not to chase birds!'

Timothy dashed along the sand for a while, splashing in and out of the little seawater puddles left by the tide. Then he sat down, staring up at the departing birds. How dare they fly away! How was a puppy supposed to catch them if they took off into the sky? Looking sulky he turned and ran back to George. She gave him a quick hug. 'Never mind, Timmy, I'm not really angry with you.' She threw him another stick and he chased after it happily.

They were having such a lovely game, running, jumping, skipping and hopping and so pleased to be out in the fresh air on such a lovely day, that George hardly noticed they had reached the end of the beach. They were close to the large rocks at the base of the headland, further along than she had ever been before.

Timothy had abandoned his stick and was scrambling around the rocks, hunting in the pools and sniffing everything exciting there was to sniff.

George went after him, slipping and sliding across to a shallow pool full of tiny shrimps and fish. Limpets were stuck to the side of the rocks and a scarlet sea-anemone waved its fronds as the water moved to and fro. Timothy was sitting down with his head cocked to one side, watching it intently. What on earth was this strange, colourful creature that was silly enough to live under the water?

'What have you found, Timmy, darling?' asked George when she reached him. 'Ooh, a sea-anemone! Isn't it beautiful!'

They sat watching until Timothy became bored and scrambled away. Soon he had clambered right round the headland and was standing waiting for George to catch up.

'Phew!' said George as she reached him. She had slipped several times and the bottom of her jeans was stained green with seaweed. She stood with her hands on her hips staring at the wide expanse of rocky shore in front of her. 'I've never been this far before, Timmy. We are having an exciting time!'

Suddenly George noticed something even more thrilling. Just along from where they were standing was a cave set deep into the cliff. 'Gosh, Timmy, look at that!' she cried. 'Let's go and explore, shall we?'

The little girl's heart drummed with excitement as she and her puppy dashed across to the cave mouth. What a wonderful thing to find. They stood at the entrance, peering into the deep, dark, gloomy interior. She imagined herself and Timothy as brave explorers on the verge of an important and exciting discovery.

'Right, Timmy,' said George, stepping bravely forward. 'Let's go inside, shall we?'

It was even more mysterious and exciting inside the cave than it had looked from the outside. The floor was littered with large boulders and the walls gave off a curious, pinky glow. Pools of water reflected the high, rugged ceiling.

The cave was huge, so huge George could not see the end of it.

'Goodness!' said George, her eyes round with wonder and surprise. 'What brilliant fun, Timmy! This is almost as eerie as my castle.'

'Wuff,' agreed Timothy, sniffing around to find out if he could smell any cave monsters, his plumy tail waving in the air. He gave an excited little bark. There was a strange smell here but he could not work out what it was.

George stared at the ceiling, wondering if there were any gulls' nests high up on the rocky ledges. Timothy scampered off towards the gloomy depths of the back of the cave. George hurried after him.

'Timmy! Timmy! Where are you?' called George. The sound of her voice bounced off the walls and came echoing eerily back towards her. She gave a little shiver of excitement. This really was the best fun she had had for ages.

Then, to George's surprise, another sound began to echo around. An odd, ghostly sound, like a bell ringing from way above her head. It came again, then was followed by a strange banging noise and a weird, echoing squeak and a swishing, swooshing kind of noise that sent shivers down George's spine.

Timothy began barking his head off and running round to try to smell where the noises were coming from. The fur on the back of his neck was standing on end and he was very excited.

'Timmy, come here!' called George, bending down to scoop him up in her arms. Her heart drummed in her chest and she gave another little shiver. This time she felt just a little afraid. 'What was it, Timmy? Was it a ghost?'

Timothy pricked up his ears at the word 'ghost'. He licked the freckles on George's nose. If it was a ghost then he was not a bit scared. His duty was to protect his mistress. He gave another bark and a small whine as George hugged him close. She was quite determined not to be frightened. The noises had probably just been the sea breeze blowing in and out of the cave and the sound of the waves breaking on the rocks. Anyway, she thought to herself bravely, only girls get scared.

George and Timothy made their way back out to the cave entrance. George looked round. There was no sign of anything that could have made those strange noises. She really had no idea what it could be.

The tide had come in now and it would not be long before it was impossible to get round the headland back to the Kirrin side of the beach.

'Come on, Timmy!' called George, jumping from rock to rock. 'Let's go and tell Mummy all about the cave . . . and the ghost!'

8

Timothy in trouble

At Kirrin Cottage it was almost lunch-time. George was very pleased as her stomach had been rumbling all the way home. The fresh air and all the excitement had given her an enormous appetite. Finding the cave really was the most thrilling thing to happen.

Joanna was in the kitchen preparing the meal.

'Where's Mummy?' demanded George, going in with Timothy. 'I've got something terrifically exciting to tell her.'

'She's in the lounge with two policemen,' said Joanna. 'So don't you go disturbing them.'

'Policemen!' exclaimed George. 'What do they want Mummy for?'

'They've come about the post office robbery,' said Joanna, busily peeling the potatoes. 'They want to know if we saw anything suspicious that evening.'

'Oh,' said George, taking Timothy's bag of food from the cupboard and putting some into his bowl with a dish of fresh water beside it. 'Well, we didn't.'

'I think that's what your mother's telling them,' said Joanna.

Timothy had just finished gobbling up his food when George's mother and two burly police officers came through into the kitchen.

'This is George,' said her mother, introducing the two officers.

'Hello, son,' said the taller of the two. 'We've been making enquiries about the post office robbery. Did you see any strangers hanging around in the village yesterday?'

George grinned and felt very well-disposed to the policeman who had called her 'son'.

'She's actually my daughter,' said her mother hastily. 'Her real name's Georgina.'

George's smile turned into a scowl as the two policemen laughed.

'You look like a boy to me,' the other, shorter policeman said, eyeing her tousled hair, dirty jeans and scuffed shoes.

'Thank you,' said George haughtily. 'That's just what I want to look like. I hate being a girl.'

'That's enough, dear,' said her mother patiently. 'Could you just answer the officer's question please? I'm sure they've got better things to do than standing here discussing whether you're a boy or a girl.'

'Sorry, Mummy,' said George, thinking for a moment. 'No, sorry,' she said. 'I didn't see anyone suspicious in the village at all. I wish I had, though, it would have been really thrilling. I was too busy trying to find out who owned Timmy.' She was going to pick the puppy up to show the policemen but the little dog had scampered back into the hall.

'Well,' said the tall officer. 'If any of you remember anything at all perhaps you'd ring the police station. I'm sorry your husband can't be disturbed but maybe you could ask him when he comes out of his study.'

'Yes, certainly, I will,' said George's mother, showing them out. 'I hope Mrs Wood has recovered from the shock of the break-in.'

'Yes, she's fine,' said the officer, 'although she's very worried about . . .' His voice faded as Mother accompanied the policemen to the gate.

'Poor woman,' remarked Joanna. 'I'd be so upset if something like that happened to me.'

'Yes,' said George. 'All that money getting stolen. It was probably some old people's savings.'

'I'm sure it was,' said Joanna, putting the potatoes on to boil.

George hovered by the door. She wished her mother would

hurry back, she was dying to tell her about the mysterious and exciting cave.

Suddenly there was a loud bang and a shout. It was Father and he was very annoyed about something.

'That wretched dog!' he shouted. 'Georgina! Come and get this dog of yours immediately.'

George threw Joanna a horrified glance. What on earth had Timothy been up to? She ran out of the kitchen and along the hall. Halfway, she met Timmy hurtling in the opposite direction. He had one of Father's slippers in his mouth and George could see the back of it was all chewed to pieces.

She turned round and ran after him. Timothy had dashed into the kitchen and was hiding beneath the table. Joanna was on her knees trying to shoo him out. Father's slipper, torn and tattered, lay between his front paws. Timothy's tail wagged uncertainly. The tall man's yell had scared him to death. He could not understand what he had done wrong. He was allowed to chew on bits of driftwood. Why was he not allowed to chew this funny-shaped piece of leather he had found at the bottom of the coat-stand?

George crawled under the table and snatched the slipper away. 'Oh, Timmy,' she said quietly. 'I'm afraid you're really in for it now.'

Her father stormed into the kitchen. 'Where's my slipper?' he shouted.

'Here,' said George in a small voice, holding up the chewed article.

'My best pair!' scowled the angry man. 'Ruined!'

'What's happened?' asked George's mother, coming in the back door after seeing the policemen off at the gate. She saw the slipper and her husband's angry face and Timothy hiding under the table. 'Oh, dear. You are supposed to be keeping an eye on him, George.'

'Sorry,' said George. 'Please don't be angry with Timmy, he didn't know it was your slipper.'

Her father had bent down and hauled Timothy out from under the table. George held her breath. If he spotted the chewed rug as well, Timothy would certainly be out on his ear.

'This dog stays outside from now on,' said her father angrily. 'If he chews things he'll have to live in the garden shed where he can't do any damage.'

'He can't,' wailed George. 'He'll hate it outside. He'll be lonely and unhappy . . . please, Father!'

Her father shook his head. 'I said you could keep him here for a month if you trained him to behave himself,' he insisted.

'Quentin,' said George's mother, putting a soothing hand on her irate husband's arm. 'He's only been here a short while. It takes weeks to train a puppy.'

Her husband seemed to calm down a little. 'Yes, I know,' he said. 'But I can't have him indoors destroying things. When you've trained him properly, Georgina, I'll think about letting him into the house again.'

'If he has to stay outside then I will too,' cried George. 'So there!'

'Oh, no, you will not, young lady,' shouted George's father. 'You'll sit and have your lunch with us. Then you may go back outside with your dog.'

When Father was in that kind of mood everyone knew it was no good arguing!

Sulkily, George took Timothy out into the garden. 'Stay here, Timmy,' she said, sitting him down by the back door. 'I promise I won't be long.'

'Wuff,' said Timothy unhappily. He lay down by the step and looked at his little mistress from under his shaggy eyebrows. 'Wuff, wuff.'

George went back indoors. She washed her hands and went to sit at the dinner table looking very sulky indeed. She had a dark frown on her brow and her eyes looked like thunder. She almost refused to eat anything but then her hunger got the better of her. Her parents sat in silence. It seemed as if there was a black cloud over the tops of their heads. Secretly George's mother thought it was a storm in a teacup. Puppies always chewed things and they could easily get Quentin another pair of slippers.

While she was eating, George was hatching a plan. She had not even had the chance to tell her parents about the cave. Now it could be her secret. If Timothy wasn't allowed in the house, then she would not live there either. She would pack up a bag and they would both go and live in the cave. There would be nothing for Timothy to chew there that would upset anyone. They would be secret and adventurous cave dwellers and no-one would ever see them again!

9

The runaways

As soon as she had finished her meal, George ran outside to find Timothy. He was sitting by the back door looking very sorry for himself. She sat down beside him and quickly whispered her plan in his ear.

'We'll wait until tonight,' said the little girl. 'The tide will be out again then and we'll be able to get to the cave. We'll take lots of food and some warm clothes and live there. We'll have a splendid adventure. All right, Timmy?' She gave the naughty puppy a big hug. 'Never you mind, Timmy, I love you dearly even if Father doesn't.'

George stayed outside with her dog until tea-time, then, after tea, she went back outside with him until it was bedtime. Mother brought Timothy's blanket out to her. 'You can make a nice snug bed in the shed for Timmy,' she said, looking at her daughter sorrowfully. 'I'm sorry, George, but you know what Father's like.'

George was so angry and upset she could not speak. She really wanted to put her arms round her mother's waist and say she was sorry and promise to keep an eye on Timmy in future but she was far too proud to do that. Instead she just took the blanket without a word, moved the wheelbarrow to one side, and made a nest with it in the corner of the shed. It was a well-built shed and not at all draughty, so she knew Timothy would not be cold even though she had insisted to Father that he would be. She took the puppy for a last run around the garden before taking him into the shed.

'Sit down on here,' she said, gently patting the blanket nest. Then she added in a whisper, 'I'll be back later so don't worry.'

Timothy watched with big, sad brown eyes as George went out and closed the door behind her. It was already getting dark and a full moon shone like a huge, shiny penny in the navy blue sky. He gave a little whine and lay down with his nose between his paws. This really was a strange household. First he slept in the kitchen. Then he was allowed to sleep upstairs with his mistress and now he had been banished to the shed. The world of humans was a very strange one indeed.

George refused to say goodnight to anyone at all and stamped up the stairs to bed much earlier than usual. Curled up under the covers she thought of all the ways she could make her father feel sorry for being so unfair and decided running away was the best way of all. Father would be really sorry when he never saw her ever again.

Instead of undressing, George had put her pyjamas on over her clothes and now lay under the covers, her heart thumping with excitement. She stayed there, wide-awake, listening to the sound of the sea until her parents were both in bed. Then she crept out of bed to pack her bag. She soon had everything she needed: a blanket from the airing cupboard, two pairs of socks and a thick jacket in case it got cold at night, her torch, some string, a penknife and a box of matches. Down the stairs she went, lugging the bag in her arms. She slipped quietly into the kitchen. There she stuffed the bag to the brim with all the goodies she could find. A packet of biscuits, a huge bag of crisps, some chocolate bars, a jar of jam and some bread, a bottle of fizzy lemonade, and Timmy's bag of puppy food. By now, the bag was so heavy she was not sure she could carry it all the way along to the cave.

'If it's too heavy,' she decided to herself, 'I'll leave some things by the path then go back for them.'

Before she left, George wrote a note to her parents. 'I have run away with Timmy,' she scribbled. 'If he is not allowed in the house then I will not live here either. Please don't worry about us, we shall be quite safe.' She signed it 'George' without any kisses so they would know how angry and upset she was.

Outside, Timothy was waiting eagerly in the shed. He had heard George creeping about and knew she was coming to rescue him. He jumped up at her as soon as she opened the door.

The little girl held a finger to her lips. Her heart was pounding more than ever. This was another gloriously thrilling adventure. What luck she and Timothy had found the cave, otherwise when she decided to run away she would not have known where to go.

George collected her fishing rod from the back of the shed then, together, the two runaways tiptoed out of the back gate and down the narrow path that led to the bay. The full moon made the night almost as bright as day as the two small figures hurried along. The tide was on its way out and it was not long before George and Timothy were clambering over the rocks to the mouth of the cave. George had managed to haul the heavy bag all the way there. She was determined not to be weak and silly. It was nothing to a brave cave-dweller to have to carry a heavy bag such a long way.

Past the wet floor of the smaller cave they went, making their way through the passage to the larger cave at the back.

George soon found a suitable place and dumped the bag down on the rocks. Timothy was running around excitedly. This was the fourth place he was to sleep in two days. What an exciting life for a small dog!

When she had made camp, George sat down with Timothy

beside her. She listened for a moment just in case the ghostly noises came again. Although she was only a little bit afraid she hoped there would not be any peculiar noises in the dark of the night.

All George could hear, though, was the pounding of the waves on the rocks and a small whistle now and then as the night breeze blew in the entrance and out again.

'Here you are, Timmy,' she said, giving the puppy a whole chocolate cream biscuit all to himself. A rather strange midnight feast but simply gorgeous when you have it in a secret cave. 'I'll catch some fish in the morning and we can make a fire and cook them for lunch,' added George, her mouth watering at the thought.

'Wurf,' said Timothy, thinking that sounded great fun.

Between them they polished off the biscuits and the big bag of crisps. Timothy settled down beside George and gave a huge puppy yawn. He had had so many adventures he was very tired and his tummy was very full. Soon he gave a big sigh and began to doze.

George settled herself comfortably beside a big rock and lay down next to him. Her eyes began to close. She could hardly wait for morning to come. After she had caught some fish she would try to find some dry driftwood at the back of the cave to make a fire. What fun they were going to have!

She had not been dozing for long when she suddenly heard

Timothy give a low growl. He sat bolt upright, his ears pricked and the fur on the back of his neck standing on end. George sat up too, straining her eyes in the darkness.

'What's up, Timmy?' she whispered. 'What have you heard? Is it that funny ghost again?'

Timothy's growls were really fierce for such a small puppy. All at once George saw what had disturbed him. A tall, dark figure was standing at the entrance to the cave. Its outline was black against the moonlit sky. George put her hand on Timothy's neck and drew him back behind the big rock.

'Don't growl, Timmy, darling,' she hissed.

The little dog always knew what George was saying so he stopped at once. He crouched, quivering with anger. Who on earth was snooping around their secret cave in the middle of the night? How dare they disturb them!

George was very worried. Surely it couldn't be Father hunting for her? They had left both her parents fast asleep and they would not discover that she had run away until the morning.

Timothy was still shaking and could not help giving another ferocious growl so George put her hand gently over his muzzle. 'Ssh!' she hissed. Her heart was beating loudly and she felt quite as frightened as she had ever been in her life.

They watched as the dark figure began to make its way towards them. Suddenly a light flashed as the intruder snapped on a powerful torch and shone the beam all around. It lit up the way into the larger cave where George and Timothy were hiding. George shrank back even further, trying to make herself as small as possible.

As the figure came closer, she could see it was a burly man dressed in a black leather jacket.

He had a shock of black hair and thick eyebrows that met together in the middle. He carried something under his arm but George could not make out what it was.

Suddenly Timothy could not contain himself any longer. He did not like this strange, dark figure who was trespassing in his cave. His mistress might be in danger and he knew he had to protect her. He simply had to bark and bark until he scared the man away.

The puppy was just about to lunge forward when a strange sound came from above. A whistling, ringing sound and a loud swoosh and whoosh in the darkness of the cave roof. The figure gave a loud exclamation of fear and dropped the torch. The light went out and the whole cave was plunged into sudden and utter darkness!

Timothy was so surprised that he forgot he was going to bark and sat back down beside George and allowed her to put her hand over his muzzle once more. Then the ghostly sound came again, echoing round the cave walls and up to the ceiling.

George heard the man swear as he felt around for the torch in the darkness. He found it and tried to click it on but it had hit a rock and the switch was broken. Suddenly there was a louder ringing sound and a louder swoosh and the man gave a cry and began waving his arms around his head. Then he turned and ran back the way he had come as fast as his long legs would carry him.

George heard him swearing and shouting as he scrambled over the rocks and disappeared. Then everything went quiet.

Whatever ghostly presence had scared the sinister figure away had now completely disappeared.

'Phew!' said George, giving a huge sigh of relief. 'Thank goodness he's gone. He didn't look a nice sort of person at all.' She let go of Timothy and he ran around sniffing. He came back to George and deposited something at her feet. It was the intruder's torch, well and truly broken.

George hardly slept at all after that. The appearance of the dark figure and the ghostly noises had been pretty terrifying. Even though she and Timothy settled back down on the blanket and covered themselves with her jacket she found it hard to stop thinking about it.

Who or what was making those strange, ghostly noises? She couldn't help giving a little shiver when she remembered them.

More mysterious still, who could the sinister-looking figure be and why had he come to this remote and secret cave in the middle of the night?

10

Timmy finds treasure

It was very early indeed when George and Timothy woke up from a restless doze. At first, the little girl wondered where she was. She could hear the sound of the sea much louder than she could from her bedroom up in the roof at Kirrin Cottage. She could feel the salty breeze blowing on her face.

George sat up suddenly. Of course! She had run away with Timothy and they were secret cave-dwellers!

But where was Timothy? He had completely disappeared.

George jumped to her feet. 'Timmy! Timmy! Where are you?' she called loudly.

She heard an answering bark right from the back of the cave. It was rather gloomy and mysterious back there. There was a damp feeling in the air that sent shivers down George's spine. She was glad she had made her bed closer to the entrance.

Timothy was behind a rock digging like mad. Showers of sand

and shingle flew up in the air as the puppy's claws dug deeply into the ground.

When George reached him he gazed up at her for a second or two, panting and smiling, his plumy tail waving to and fro. Then he put his shaggy head down and began digging again.

'Timmy! What have you found?' exclaimed George, kneeling down beside him.

She saw what the puppy had uncovered. It was a large tin box. Written on the side in black letters were the words 'Cash Box – Property of the Post Office'.

George gave a surprised gasp. What on earth was such a thing doing at the back of their cave? Then, all at once she realized what it was. It was the cash box that had been stolen from Mrs Wood's post office! The robber had hidden it here!

'Timmy!' exclaimed the little girl excitedly. 'We've found the stolen money . . . Oh!' George's hand flew to her mouth as she realized something else. 'That man must have been the robber coming to get his loot! When he crashed his motorbike after the robbery he must have run here and hidden the tin.'

'Woof!' said Timothy, agreeing with his mistress as usual.

George felt so excited she stood up and ran around the cave jumping and laughing with delight. 'We're so clever to have found it, aren't we, Tim?'

'Wuff,' said Timothy, still busily digging even though the cash tin was completely exposed by now. 'Wuff, wuff,' he added as if to say, 'Yes, we most certainly are!'

George came back and grasped hold of the tin. She heaved it out of the hole then sat back on her heels. 'Well done, Timmy!

You're a hero!' She gave him a big hug. 'We'd better go home and tell Mummy and Father,' she added, forgetting her parents were not supposed to be seeing her and Timothy ever again.

Before they left, the two adventurers dragged the heavy tin to a new hiding place.

'If the robber comes back for it, he won't be able to find it,' panted George when the tin was well and truly wedged behind a rock and she had covered up the grooves it had made in the sand. 'Those ghostly noises in the dark scared him away but he's bound to come back in daylight,' she added.

When they reached the mouth of the cave they saw the tide was still high and it wasn't possible to get around the rocks. George watched the waves breaking in plumes of foamy white with dismay.

'We'll have to wait a while, Timmy,' she said. Then a rumbling tummy reminded her they had not had their breakfast. 'Never mind. We'll have a picnic first. If we can't get out, then the robber can't get in, can he?'

'Wurf,' said Timothy, pleased they were going to eat before they hurried back to Kirrin Cottage. After all, digging made a puppy very hungry indeed!

By now, the sun had risen and it was another lovely blue day with just a hint of cotton-wool clouds drifting lazily past.

George perched on the rocks close to the cave entrance, dangling her bare feet in one of the warm pools. She was eating slices of bread spread with jam, biscuits and crisps and drinking lemonade. This was heaven!

George had forgotten to bring a cup so she drank the lemonade straight from the bottle. It tasted much better that way. She hadn't remembered to bring a bowl for Timothy either so she found a large, flat rock with a hollow in the centre. Timothy thought it made a lovely dog bowl even if it did make the food taste a little salty.

'Isn't this exciting!' exclaimed George, her blue eyes glowing with excitement. 'I wish we could stay here for ever.' Then she gave another sigh. 'I suppose everyone will have to know our secret now we've found the stolen money. Oh well, perhaps when Father hears how clever you've been, Timmy, he'll let you back into the house and we shan't need to be cave-dwellers after all. Even though it would have been terrific!'

Timothy gave a small bark and licked her nose. He liked it here but it was definitely more comfortable sleeping on his mistress's bed. After all, that was a secret too, wasn't it?

By the time they had finished their picnic breakfast, the tide had receded far enough for them to clamber across the rocks and run home.

At Kirrin Cottage, Father was in his study and Mother had gone out shopping. Joanna was in the kitchen washing up the breakfast things.

'Your mother said you were to have breakfast in here when you came back from your walk,' said Joanna as George and Timothy hurtled in the back door. 'And she said to warn you that your father was not to be disturbed.'

'Oh, blow!' exclaimed George, completely forgetting for a minute that she had left a note telling them she had run away. Then she remembered it and saw with a sigh of relief that it was lying under the chair by the stove. It must have blown off the table when someone opened the back door so no-one had seen it. Mummy must have thought she had simply taken Timmy out for an early walk.

'When will Mummy be back?' asked George, going to pick up the note and screwing it up and throwing it in the fire. 'I've got something awfully important to tell her.'

'She's gone shopping and to have morning coffee with some new people in the village,' replied the housekeeper. 'I don't know when she'll be back, I'm afraid.'

'But, Joanna!' exclaimed George. 'We've found the money stolen from the post office. I've simply got to tell her!'

Joanna laughed. 'Oh, George, you are funny. You're having such a lovely time playing pretend games with that puppy. I'm so glad you found him, you know. I always thought you were such a lonely little girl . . .'

'But it's true,' insisted George. 'We're not making it up!'

Joanna gave another smile and bent down to stroke Timothy. 'What would you like for your breakfast, little dog? Would you like some toast for a change?'

George gave a little snort of annoyance. 'Well, if you won't believe me I'll jolly well have to go and find someone who does!' she said angrily. 'Come on, Timmy!'

Timothy followed her outside looking a little disappointed at not being allowed to have two breakfasts.

George went to sit on her garden swing to think things out. Sitting on a swing out in the fresh sea air often helped you think if you had a great problem to solve.

'It's no good disturbing Father,' said George, knowing he hated disobedience. 'He'll be terribly cross and won't listen to a thing we've got to say.'

'Wurf,' said Timothy, agreeing with her.

'And waiting for Mummy is just wasting time,' said George.

Timothy didn't seem to hear what she had said this time. He ran into the garden shed and grabbed hold of the corner of the blanket. He was bored with talking and wanted to play a game. He pulled the blanket out of the door, growling and shaking it.

George jumped off the swing. 'Timmy, there's no time for games, we've got terribly important things to think about!' she cried.

'Grrr,' growled Timothy, shaking the blanket even harder.

George ran to rescue it from his sharp little teeth. It was an old blanket but even so Mummy wouldn't be very pleased if it got ripped.

The more George pulled at the blanket though, the more the puppy thought it was a wonderful game. At last she managed to get it away from him, but not before the corner was torn and tattered. She folded it up with the tear inside and took it back into the shed. She hoped Timothy wouldn't have to sleep on it any more when Father heard how clever and brave he had been but she had better put it somewhere safe, just in case.

In the shed, George's eye fell upon the wheelbarrow. Suddenly the little girl's face brightened and a huge grin spread across her face. A marvellous idea had just come into her head.

'Timmy!' she called as the puppy ran off to find something else to play with. 'Come here, I've just had the most thrilling idea! We'll take the wheelbarrow and fetch the cash tin back here. Then everyone will have to believe we've found it, won't they, darling Timmy?'

'Wuff,' said Timothy happily. Another run round the bay! Living here with George was the best thing that ever happened to a dog!

George quickly wheeled the barrow through the gate. Along the narrow path to the cove they went, down the slope to the shore.

Timothy gambolled on ahead. Once or twice he ran back, biting and barking at the squeaky wheel of the barrow. He was practising being a fierce, grown-up dog protecting his mistress from things that made strange noises. He wished he had been able to bite the strange creature that had made those noises in the cave but he hadn't been able to see it anywhere.

George giggled at the puppy's antics. 'Careful, Timmy,' she cried. 'You'll get run over!'

It was very hard to push the barrow across the wet sand. Once or twice the wheel got stuck and Timothy barked encouragement as George pulled and pushed and heaved.

By the time they reached the rocky headland, the tide was a long way out. George dragged the heavy barrow from one rock to another and at last they were at the cave entrance.

George stopped, looking inside warily for new footprints in the sand. Then she heaved a sigh of relief. 'No-one's been here since we left, Tim,' she said. 'So the robber hasn't been back yet. We'd better get a move on though, he could appear at any minute.'

Timothy ran to the back of the cave just to make sure the tin was still in its new hiding place. He soon found it and stood guard while George brought the barrow round.

'Phew, Timmy,' panted George. 'This is very hard work.' She was just about to heave the heavy tin up into the wheelbarrow when there was a sound from the back of the cave. George almost jumped out of her skin as the strange noise echoed round the walls.

'Oh, blow!' she whispered to Timothy, her heart pounding like a drum. 'It's that wretched ghost again!'

Timothy was listening with his little head cocked to one side. Then suddenly he gave a most furious bark. He had had enough of this strange noise scaring his mistress. He really had to do something about it.

The little dog ran around the cave barking angrily and very fiercely. He would not let any silly old ghost interfere with their adventure.

'That's right, Timmy,' called George bravely, her heart beating like a drum. 'You scare it away!'

The noise went on and then it began to change. It started to sound like someone's shrill voice. George felt a tingle of fear. Was there a person in the cave trying to scare them off? Maybe the robber had returned after all. Was he trying to scare them away so they wouldn't identify him?

'Come on, Timmy,' called George with a shivery feeling going down her spine. 'Let's put the tin in the wheelbarrow and get home as fast as we can!'

By the time they were over the rocks and half-way home George began to think she had been rather silly. There could not possibly be such a thing as a ghost. If it had been the robber, they would have seen his footprints. Whoever, or whatever had been making those horrid sounds had only done it to scare them. As they got closer to home, it didn't seem so important. The really vital thing was to get their exciting find back to the house as soon as possible.

'What a surprise Mummy and Father are going to have when they see what we've got, Timmy, darling!' said George with glee. 'I simply can't wait to see their faces when we turn up with the stolen goods, can you?'

'Wuff!' Timothy said, running on ahead. 'Wuff, wuff!!'

11

A plan to catch a thief

George's mother was just returning with a basket full of groceries over her arm when she spotted George trundling the wheelbarrow towards her, Timothy scampering by her side.

'George!' she called, waiting by the gate. 'What on earth are you doing? And look at you, you're wet and absolutely filthy!'

When George reached her she blurted out the whole story without even taking a breath.

'And here it is, Mummy,' said the little girl triumphantly, showing her mother the cash box. 'Don't you think we're awfully clever?'

Her mother was quite taken aback. 'Are you sure this is the stolen money?' she said, gazing at the tin.

'Oh, Mummy, what else can it be?' asked George.

'Well,' said her mother. 'We had better tell your father at once.'

George's mother carried her basket into the kitchen then came back out to help George carry the tin indoors. It was very heavy, full of silver and bronze coins as well as notes and important documents.

They dumped it on the kitchen table. Joanna looked very surprised. 'What on earth have you got there?' she asked.

'The post office cash tin,' said George. 'I told you we'd found it.'

'Well, well,' said Joanna. 'And I thought you were playing a game.'

'I'll just go and tell Father,' said George's mother. 'And then we'll phone the police.'

Father came out of his study to see the tin for himself while Mother phoned the police station. It wasn't long before they heard the sound of a police car drawing up outside Kirrin Cottage and there was an urgent knock at the front door. The two police officers who had called before were standing on the doorstep when George went to open it.

'Well, Miss,' said the taller one of the two. 'Your mother tells us you have been having an adventure.'

George gave them a great big grin. 'And Timmy,' she said. 'He's the real hero, not me.'

They all went into the front room to hear George's story. Father was so surprised when he heard what she had to say that he did not even think to shoo Timothy outside. The puppy sat quietly beside George as she told everyone about the cave and the treasure and the ghost. The puppy thought perhaps if he was very quiet, and very good, the tall man called Father might let him stay indoors for ever.

'Ghost!' exclaimed Father when George told them about the strange noises. 'Don't be silly, Georgina, there's no such thing.'

'Well, something was making those noises,' insisted George, annoyed she had been called by her full name. 'We didn't imagine it, did we, Timmy?'

'Woof,' said Timothy very softly indeed.

'I'll just go and ring Mrs Wood to come and identify the cash box,' said one of the policemen. 'Then we'll take a full description of the robber from your daughter so we can send it out to all our police stations.'

'Aren't you going to try to catch the thief?' asked George.

'Yes, of course we are,' said the tall officer. 'He'll be going back to the cave to fetch the loot, I'm sure.'

'And we can lie in wait for him,' said George excitedly.

'Wuff, wuff,' said Timothy.

'Yes,' said the policeman, grinning. 'He'll get more than he bargained for when we nab him, that's for sure.'

'May we come too?' asked George eagerly. 'After all, we did find the tin.'

'Oh . . . I'm not sure about that,' said her mother dubiously.

'Oh, please, Mummy,' said George.

'Well, I don't think it will do any harm,' said the policeman kindly. 'You'll need to show us the cave anyway.'

'Oh, thanks,' said George, her eyes shining. 'This is going to be thrilling, Timmy, don't you think?'

'Wuff,' said Timothy. He couldn't wait to get to the cave to bark at that strange ghost again. And there was nothing he'd like better than to get hold of the robber's trousers and tear them to bits.

'The sooner we get along there, the better,' said the other policeman.

'Yes, said George. 'The tide will be coming in again soon so he's bound to come. If he doesn't, he'll have to wait hours before he can get into the cave again. Then it will be getting dark and I bet he'll be too scared the ghost might come again.'

'And perhaps we can solve that mystery too while we're there,' said the other policeman, smiling at George.

George's parents waited for Mrs Wood while the two police officers followed her and Timothy outside and back along the path to the beach. George pointed out where she had first seen the robber, then took the policemen round the headland and into the cave. Timothy capered on inside, running to show the policemen where he had dug up the tin.

'Don't you think Timmy's terribly clever?' asked George proudly.

'I do indeed,' said the tall policeman. 'He would make a terrific police dog.'

'Oh no,' George said as the puppy scampered back towards them. She picked him up and hugged him close. 'If no-one claims him I'm hoping Father will let me keep him for ever.'

'After this episode I should think that's very likely,' said the shorter man with a grin. 'I know I would if you were my little girl.'

They crouched down behind one of the big boulders and waited for the thief to come back. George felt sure he would have recovered from his fright by now and would soon be on the trail of his loot once more.

'No sign of that ghost of yours,' said the tall policeman in a low whisper, looking up to the high ceiling of the cave.

'It might make a noise at any time,' whispered George. 'Mightn't it, Timmy?'

Timothy whined in agreement. He could not wait for the ghost to start so he could have a jolly good bark at it.

It wasn't long before Timothy's hackles went up and he gave a low growl. He had heard the crunch and thump of footsteps round the rocks long before anyone else.

'Ssh,' hissed George, her hand on his muzzle. She turned to the policemen, her heart thumping. She could feel Timothy quivering with excitement beneath her hand. 'Someone's coming!'

Sure enough, a dark figure in a black leather jacket was outlined in the cave entrance. Everyone drew back even further into their hiding places. The policemen wanted to witness the robber hunting for the stolen money before they jumped out and arrested him.

George hardly dared to breathe as the man made his way directly towards them. He walked around the rocks to the place where he had buried the tin. He stood there for a moment with a puzzled frown on his face. He knelt down, staring at the hole where the cash tin had been. Then he began digging frantically with his bare hands and swearing in a very loud voice indeed.

This was enough for the policemen. They both gave a shout and jumped out from their hiding place.

'That's enough, my man,' shouted the tall officer. 'You're coming with us!'

The robber gave them a shocked and startled glance, then leapt to his feet and ran back to the cave entrance as fast as he could, with the policemen in hot pursuit.

George released Timothy and he dived after all three men, dodging round the heavy-footed policemen and catching up with the robber. He grasped the hem of the man's trousers in his teeth and began growling and shaking, trying to halt him in his tracks.

'Get off, you lousy dog!' shouted the man, kicking out at

Timothy. But the puppy would not let go. As the man's leg rose in the air, Timothy rose with it, still growling, all four paws off the ground.

George gasped. Timothy could well be injured if the man's kick landed on him. But the puppy was too clever and clung to the man's trouser leg like a limpet until he had to stop trying to run and bend to pull him off.

Just as the man skidded to a halt there was another surprise in store.

With a loud squawk and a squeak, something swooped down from a ledge close to the ceiling in a flash of red and green. It landed on the man's head and inflicted a very hard peck on his scalp. He yelled in fear, his arms going like windmills. George gasped in surprise. It was Mrs Wood's parrot from the post office! What on earth was it doing here?

The policemen had got hold of the robber now and were wrestling him to the ground. Timothy let go of his trouser leg and ran back to George with a piece of black material dangling from his mouth. He laid it at her feet then looked up at her, grinning, his tongue lolling out. She reached down and scooped him up in her arms. 'Well done, Timmy!' she cried, smothering him with kisses. 'You're absolutely wonderful! And look, there's our ghost. It was Mrs Wood's parrot all the time!'

As the officers tackled the robber, the parrot flew off again, finally settling on a jagged piece of rock not far above George and Timothy.

'Ding dong,' it shrieked. 'Pretty young lady!'

George tried to scowl. Pretty young lady indeed! What an insult! But she was so excited that the robber had been caught she couldn't manage a scowl. So she laughed instead and called out to the parrot. 'Come on, Polly, I'll take you home to your mistress.'

But the parrot would not come down. It simply stayed up there, muttering and murmuring sadly to itself. George felt quite sorry for the poor creature. It had been lost in the cave for two days and did not know where it was.

By now, her parents and Mrs Wood were hurrying along the shore towards the cave. Mrs Wood had identified the cash box and now they were anxious to see if the thief had been caught. The policemen passed them, each holding firmly on to one arm of their prisoner. 'We'll take him to the station then come back for your statements,' they told everyone.

Mrs Wood didn't know which event to be the most pleased about. She was very relieved that the money had been found and the robber caught but even more overjoyed that her dear old parrot was safe and sound.

'He escaped when the robber turned everything upside down,'

she explained when the parrot was safely sitting on her shoulder squawking and muttering with joy at finding his mistress once again. 'The cage door sprang open and he flew off in fright,' added Mrs Wood. 'I'm so pleased to have him back.'

'Pretty Polly,' the parrot murmured in his mistress's ear. 'Dong, dong, lady.'

'We thought he was a ghost,' admitted George with a grin. 'We were jolly scared, I can tell you.'

'Well, I think you've been awfully brave,' said her father. 'And my word, that puppy of yours has been surprisingly fearless too!'

'Oh, Father, do you really think so?' cried George. 'Please could he come back in the house, then? I promise to keep an eye on him.'

Father gave his wife a glance and she smiled and nodded. 'Very well, George,' he said.

'Oh, thank you, Father!' The little girl ran to give her father a great big hug. The tall man hugged her back. Although he was very strict and stern he loved his fierce little daughter with all his heart and admired her bravery and spirit.

'Mind you,' he added. 'If he's naughty again he's out on his ear.'

George looked up at her father. 'Oh, he won't be,' she promised, keeping her fingers crossed behind her back. 'Honestly.'

George and her little dog skipped on ahead of Mother, Father, Mrs Wood and the parrot. 'Maybe Father will even let you stay for ever if no-one comes for you,' she said to the puppy when they were out of earshot. 'Oh, Timmy, darling, wouldn't that be thrilling? We could have lots and lots more adventures together.'

'Wurf,' agreed Timothy happily. Staying with George and having lots of exciting adventures would be the very best thing a puppy could ever do!

ADVENTURE
FACTS
GUIDE

WHICH DOG IS BEST FOR YOU?

A dog is likely to be part of the family for 10 to 15 years, so it's important to choose your breed carefully. Do your homework before you go to look for a puppy, because it's all too easy to fall in love with a dog who may not be right for you. Here are some things to think about before you make your decision.

SIZE

Puppies are cute and cuddly, but they soon grow bigger – sometimes much bigger.

If you live in a house or flat with small rooms, think about how much space your fully-grown dog will take up. Don't forget that your pet will have to fit into your car, too. Large dogs often have a shorter life span than smaller breeds, and they are more expensive to feed and insure.

Dogs come in all shapes and sizes, so there's an ideal canine companion for everyone.

EXERCISE

Some breeds, such as pointers, collies and setters, are naturally full of energy because they've been bred for hunting or herding sheep. These intelligent and lively dogs need a lot of exercise, otherwise they soon become unhappy and overweight – and it won't be long before they're using their excess energy to get into mischief. Be realistic about the amount of exercise your family will be able to offer a dog. If you prefer chilling in front of the TV to hiking in the hills, dogs that enjoy the lazier lifestyle include bulldogs, dachshunds, pugs and Yorkshire terriers.

GROOMING

All dogs need regular grooming and this can be a good way to bond with your pet, but think twice before taking on a long-haired breed. Dogs with long coats need grooming every day, otherwise their fur quickly becomes matted and tangled.

Pugs like to run around and have fun, but they are happy to relax too.

OTHER PETS

If you already have a dog, think about how your pet will adapt to a newcomer – some are happier to be the only dog in the family. If you decide to go ahead, try to introduce the two dogs away from your home, so your dog doesn't see the puppy as an intruder. Make sure your adult dog has some quiet time and extra attention, away from the puppy, and never leave a puppy alone with an adult dog.

It may take some time, but dogs and cats can become the best of friends.

Cats and dogs should be introduced to one another gradually. A cat's reaction to a puppy will be to run away, and the puppy will think it's great fun to chase the cat. Make sure that your cat can escape to a higher level, out of reach of the dog, and feed both animals separately. Terriers have been bred to chase small animals, so if you own a cat, a terrier may not be the best breed for you.

This Old English sheepdog looks adorable, but imagine trying to clean him up when he's been playing in the mud.

HOW TO LOOK AFTER YOUR PUPPY

A BASIC GUIDE

Looking after a puppy is a huge responsibility; all dogs need frequent exercise, regular meals, training, grooming, playtime and sometimes even trips to the vet – puppies need these things even more.

If you have thought about it carefully, and decided that you are able to offer your puppy everything that he needs, then this guide will help you to make your home a warm and welcoming place for your new friend.

CREATE YOUR 'PUPPY SPACE'

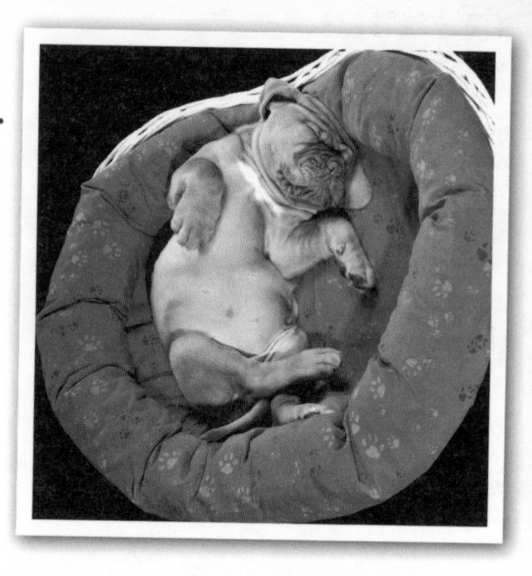

Your 'puppy space' is an area of your home that is just for your puppy; usually a corner of your kitchen, utility room or entrance hall. Giving your puppy this space will help him to feel safe, and will also give you a smaller area to have to clear up if he has any accidents!

PUPPY-PROOF YOUR HOME

Puppies love to chew; they don't do it to be naughty, they are just playful and have growing teeth! There is a special non-biting fluid available that you can put on things to stop them being bitten, but chew toys are the best solution for stopping your new dog from chewing the leg on Mum's antique chair, or Dad's favourite slipper!

PROVIDE FOR YOUR PUPPY

Make sure you have all the things that your puppy needs before bringing him home. A comfy bed is very important, and for very young dogs a ticking clock wrapped in a blanket can remind them of their mother's heartbeat and make them feel calmer – just make sure it's not an alarm clock set to go off! You will also need two bowls – one for food, and one for water; a brush is important, especially if your dog has long hair as you will need to help him out with all those tangles. Puppies also love to play, so your new friend would appreciate a couple of toys to play with when you aren't around for games.

STOP BAD HABITS BEFORE THEY START

Just like little children, puppies like to test the boundaries. You are in charge, so it is your job to make sure that your puppy knows those boundaries, and that they are firm. It can be very hard to do when your new friend looks up at you with those big eyes ... but if you let him get away with things now he'll never learn to do what you ask. A basic obedience class can help with mischievous dogs, or if you just need some hints and tips on basic puppy training.

SAFETY GUIDELINES FOR EXPLORING CAVES

ADVENTURE FACTS GUIDE

Caves are exciting and mysterious, but they can be dangerous places too, so make sure you follow these guidelines before you start exploring.

Always go in a team of at least four people, including two adults. Then, if someone is injured, one person can stay with the casualty, while the other two go for help.

All members of the group must stay within hearing distance of one another.

Let people know where you are going and when you expect to be back, so they can alert the emergency services in case of trouble.

Most caves are carved out by water, so they could become flooded, trapping people inside.

Heavy rain can submerge an inland cave, and sea caves may fill with water very quickly if the tide comes in. Check the weather forecast and tide tables and ask local people for advice before you enter a cave.

Sturdy clothes and footwear are a must. It will be much colder inside a cave, so take extra layers of clothing with you. Fabrics which dry quickly and are warm when wet are much better than cotton. If there is any risk of rock falls, wear a helmet, too.

Passages can look completely different viewed from another direction and even experienced cavers get lost sometimes. Mark your route with string, or leave pointers made of stones at junctions.

Take torches or headlamps with spare bulbs and batteries, a first aid kit and mobile phones (although they probably won't work inside the cave).

Caves are fragile ecosystems that can easily be damaged, so if you are exploring, respect these special environments. Don't leave anything behind but your footprints and don't take anything away from the cave.

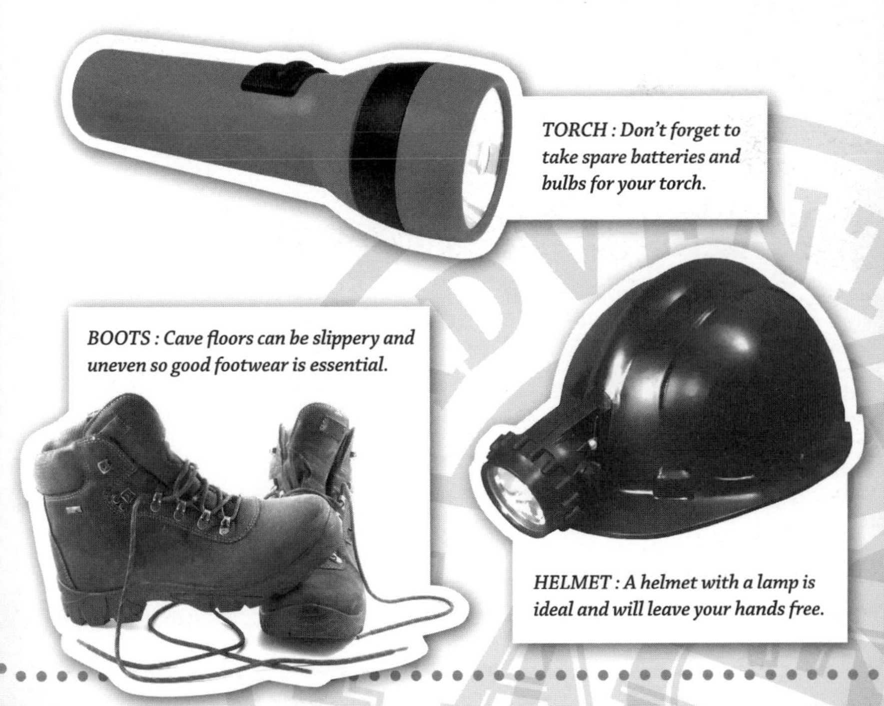

TORCH : Don't forget to take spare batteries and bulbs for your torch.

BOOTS : Cave floors can be slippery and uneven so good footwear is essential.

HELMET : A helmet with a lamp is ideal and will leave your hands free.

CAVES

People have been making use of caves since the first humans took shelter from the weather in prehistoric times. Later, pirates and smugglers used caves to stash their booty and nowadays they are often used to grow mushrooms, or age cheese or wine.

Caves can be created in several ways. Sometimes they form when large rocks get stacked up on top of one another after a landslide, but most are carved out of the rock by the action of water or form in lava from volcanoes.

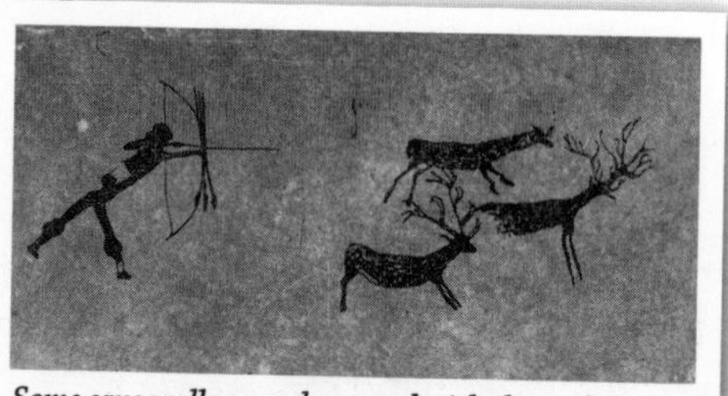

Some cave walls were decorated with the earliest-known works of art, created over 30,000 years ago.

Smugglers may have used this Cornish cave as a hiding place.

Sea caves are found all over the world and are formed when waves attack weak areas of rock in the cliff face. The longest known sea cave is the Painted Cave in California, which measures 374 metres (1,227 feet).

Lava tube caves develop when the outside of a lava stream hardens, forming a crust around the molten lava. When the lava stops flowing, the empty tube is left behind.

Most inland caves are found in limestone rock. As rainwater seeps through the soil, it gathers carbon dioxide from plant material, which turns the water into a weak solution of carbonic acid (the same acid that's in fizzy drinks). The acidic water dissolves the limestone and, as time goes by, caverns form within the rock. The water that drips through the rock into the cavern often contains minerals, which form icicle-like deposits – called stalactites – that hang from the roof. If water drips on to the floor of the cave, the minerals form stalagmites, which rise up like pillars. Sometimes stalactites and stalagmites join together to make a column.

A stalactite holds tight (tite) to the ceiling of a cave and a stalagmite might (mite) one day meet it.

Bats sleep in caves during the day and fly out to hunt at night. Bracken Cave, in Texas, is home to more than 20 million bats!

The blind cave salamander lives in the underground waters of caves in central Europe.

CAVE DWELLERS

Creatures such as bats, crickets, spiders and snails often take shelter at the entrance to a cave. They're called 'troglophiles', which means that they like living in caves but they go outside to feed.

True cave-dwellers are known as 'troglobites'. They live deep inside cave systems and spend their whole lives in the dark, so they have no need of eyes or pigment to protect their skin from sunlight. These blind salamanders, fish, shrimps, snails, spiders and millipedes are extra sensitive to sounds and smells and have other senses that react to changes in temperature and air pressure.

WHY YOU GET ECHOES

Sound travels in waves, like light, and is reflected in the same way, so an echo is heard when a sound bounces off a solid object. But why don't you hear an echo if you shout in your living room?

To get a good echo, you need to be at least 75 metres (246 feet) from a hard surface, otherwise the sound will bounce back too quickly. Sound travels at about 343 metres (1,100 feet) per second, so if you hear an echo one second after you make a sound, the echo will have bounced off a surface 171.5 metres (550 feet) away – it takes half a second to travel there and half a second to come back.

Like a ball, sound bounces at the same angle that it hits an object, so you will get a better echo from a smooth surface straight in front of you as it will travel directly back to your ear.

The sound you make needs to be loud. Sound loses energy as it travels, so the noise you hear back will be quieter.

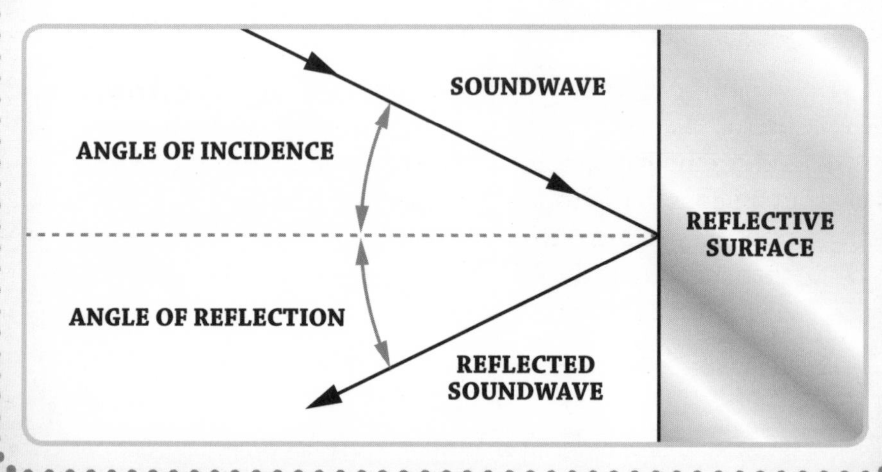

The best echoes are heard in an enclosed space, such as a big building, because there are more surfaces to bounce the noise back to you. It needs to be pretty empty because any other objects will absorb the sound. In nature, large caves with smooth walls make perfect echo chambers. Other places you might hear a good echo are deep wells, canyons or cliffs next to water.

Dolphins make clicking sounds that bounce back as an echo when they strike an object.

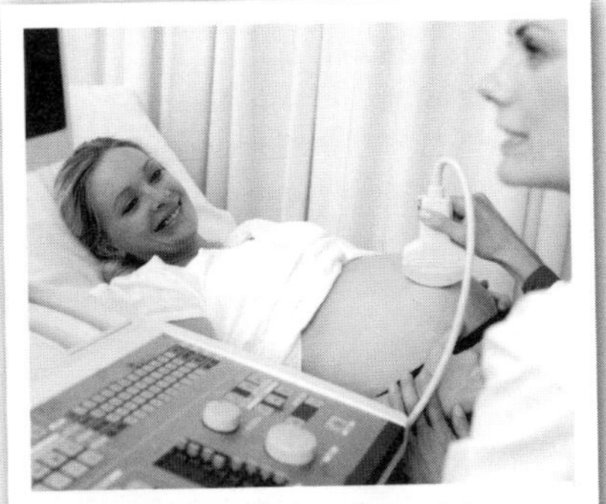

The probe is the mouth and ears of the ultrasound machine, making and receiving the sound.

Echoes are fun, but they can be very useful, too. An ultrasound-scanning machine sends out millions of pulses of high-frequency sound each second, then registers their echoes to produce an image of an unborn baby, or the body's internal organs.

Ships use sonar transmitters to send out sounds that bounce off underwater objects and return echoes to the machine's receiver. Sonar was developed to track enemy submarines during the Second World War, but now it is used to find shoals of fish and locate obstacles under the water. If the *Titanic* had been equipped with sonar, it could have avoided the iceberg that sank it. Whales, dolphins and bats use the same system to find their prey. This is called echolocation.

ROCKPOOL WILDLIFE

At low tide, rockpools reveal magical, miniature worlds, which give you a chance to study their permanent and temporary residents at close quarters.

A rockpool can be a full-time home for creatures such as limpets and anemones; for others, it's a nursery where they can shelter from the waves before they grow big enough to venture out to sea; or it might be a stopover for visitors that get trapped when the tide goes out.

Limpets cling to rocks using a suction pad and move very slowly. They have coiled, rasping tongues with thousands of tiny 'teeth' that scrape algae from the rockface.

Hermit crabs have soft bodies so they live in empty shells for protection. As they grow, they move to larger shells.

Anemones use their tentacles to attract prey such as shrimps. They are very delicate, so don't touch them.

Rockpool dwellers need fresh seawater to provide food and oxygen, so the most interesting pools are close to the low tide mark. As these are only cut off from the sea for a short time, a greater variety of species can survive there. Conditions in pools at the top of the beach are harsh and only a few of the toughest creatures can adapt to the extreme environment.

Starfish are a rare rockpool find.

Take a pocket guide to help you identify a pool's inhabitants and approach quietly, as creatures will hide if they feel threatened – look carefully as some are well camouflaged and hard to spot. In lower-shore rockpools you may find small fish, such as gobies, blennies, young pollock and wrasse, along with shrimps, prawns and sea urchins. Crabs hide in crevices, and you could come across a stranded starfish.

Remember that each part of a rockpool may be essential to the survival of one or other of its inhabitants, so if you lift a stone to see what's beneath it, put it back.

Sometimes you might be lucky enough to find a mermaid's purse. These are the empty egg cases of skates, sharks and rays, which are washed up by the sea.

TIPS TO KEEP YOU SAFE

> **Wear sensible shoes. Rocks are often slippery and it's easy to cut yourself on sharp shells.**

> **Wash your hands after handling sea creatures or seaweed.**

> **Keep an eye on the sea – you don't want to get cut off by the tide coming in.**

MYSTERY MAZE

ADVENTURE FACTS GUIDE

Can you find your way through the underground tunnels to the robbers' hiding place?

START >

FINISH >

A Curious Treasure

1

Timothy is naughty

'Timmy will be good, honestly, Father,' cried George, gazing up at her tall, rather stern parent. '*Please* let him stay!'

It had been a whole month since George, a little girl with very short, dark curly hair and vivid blue eyes, had found the stray puppy on the moor behind her house. She had asked everywhere to see if she could find the shaggy brown puppy's owner but no-one had come forward. The village policeman had told her that if he was not claimed within a month he would have to be found a new home. Now the month was up and George could not bear to be parted from him. She had been allowed to keep the puppy at home and he had become her best friend. They went everywhere together and she had even named him – Timothy.

Now it was time to decide Timothy's future and George's father was looking uncertain.

'He did chew my best slippers,' said the tall man, gazing down at his small daughter. He was very dark and extraordinary-looking with blue eyes and thick brows that frowned a lot. Exactly like George.

Father and daughter both had quick tempers and often quarrelled even though they loved one another dearly.

'But you know Timmy's only a puppy, Father,' declared George when her father mentioned the chewed slippers. 'He'll get better as he gets older.'

'And he's done puddles in the kitchen, twice,' said Father, still with a deep, dark frown on his face.

'Well, if you won't let him stay then I won't stay either,' said George angrily, trying her best *not* to lose her temper but not succeeding very well. 'He's my best friend and I won't let him go to another home. He'd hate it. Wouldn't you, Timmy, darling?' she said, bending to hug the little dog.

'Wuff,' said Timothy sadly. He could not bear to think of being parted from his beloved mistress.

'If you made friends with some of the girls in the village,' continued George's father, 'you wouldn't be lonely and need to have a dog as your best friend.'

'I'm not at all lonely,' declared George, her face going red with annoyance. 'And Timmy is the only friend I need.'

George was not like ordinary little girls. She wanted more than anything to be a boy and hated her real name of Georgina. In fact, if anyone called her that, she simply would not answer them. She always dressed in jeans or shorts and a shirt and her face, arms and legs were as brown as a hazelnut from playing out in the sunshine. She could sail and fish and climb trees, whistle and run as fast as any boy. She had even cut off her long hair so she would *look* like a boy. Boys, thought George, are much, much better than silly, babyish girls and puppies are even better!

'Wuff,' agreed Timothy, when he heard George say he was the only friend she needed. He gazed up at his small, angry mistress with his big, melting brown eyes. He thumped his shaggy tail on the floor.

'He knows every word she's saying,' said George's mother with a sigh as she came into the room. 'Really, Quentin, I think you should let the dog stay. I've got quite fond of the little chap.'

'Thanks, Mummy,' said George, giving her mother a grateful glance.

'Oh, very well, Fanny,' said George's father irritably to his wife. 'But you *must* keep him quiet and not let him chew anything else. Do you understand, Georgina?'

George scowled once again. Why did Father always forget she hated that name? But this time she was too full of happiness to be angry for more than a few seconds. The scowl quickly disappeared.

She flung her arms round her father's waist and hugged him as hard as could be.

'Oh, thank you, Father,' she cried, her eyes shining with joy.

'Wurf,' said Timothy, jumping up at her, his tail wagging nineteen to the dozen. George let her father go and scooped the puppy up in her arms. '*He's* saying thank you too,' she said, laughing.

Father patted Timothy's soft head. 'Now, mind you behave yourself,' he said, turning to go out of the door and along to his study at the other end of the house. He was working on an important scientific formula and intended writing a book about the results. 'And no noise!' he called as he went in and banged the door shut.

'Oh, Mummy, isn't that marvellous?' cried George, still hugging Timothy so tightly that the little dog could hardly breathe. 'I can keep him at Kirrin Cottage for ever and ever!'

Kirrin Cottage was the name of the old white stone house where the family lived. It was really too big to be called a cottage. It had an old wooden front door, a beautiful red rose growing up the wall and a garden full of flowers.

The house was set on top of a low cliff overlooking Kirrin Bay. Guarding the entrance to the bay was a little rocky island called Kirrin Island. On the island was a mysterious ruined castle with two tumbledown towers and a stone courtyard. George loved to play on the island amongst the wild rabbits and flocks of seagulls. She often rowed there in her little wooden boat. She adored the castle with its ruined walls that once stood strong and proud overlooking the sea, and loved playing in the towers and the old room with its ancient stone fireplace. She imagined all the exciting things that could have happened there in days gone by. She would often pretend she was a knight or a soldier defending Kirrin Bay from deadly enemies.

The cottage and the island had belonged to her mother's family for many years. None of them could imagine living anywhere else in the world.

'Right,' said George's mother when the little girl had finished hugging Timothy and put him back down on the carpet. Straightaway the naughty puppy began biting and growling at the laces of George's plimsolls. Biting shoelaces was one of his favourite games. 'That's settled then,' continued her mother, laughing at the puppy. 'Now, dear, I want you to do something for me.'

'What's that, Mummy?' asked George, giggling and moving out of Timothy's way.

'I've promised to send some things to the village jumble sale. I'd like you to go up in the attic and turn out some of your old toys,' said her mother. 'I've already found some old things that I've put in the garden shed. You can add your toys to the pile.'

'Very well,' said George, prising the puppy's teeth gently from her laces. 'Come on, Timmy, let's see what we can find.'

'Your father is working,' called Mother as the two ran helter-skelter up the stairs. 'So don't make too much noise!'

2

A strange find

'This is going to be great fun, Timmy,' said George, pushing open the little, low door that led into the attic. The attic at Kirrin Cottage was set under the sloping roof at the far end of the house and the door was so small that even George had to bend down to get through.

Timothy followed. This was a very interesting room he hadn't been in before. He ran round between the old wooden rafters hunting for smells. There were lots of different ones, all new and exciting.

First the little dog could smell spiders and ran round in between dusty suitcases and boxes packed with old clothes trying to find where they were.

There were some tremendous mouse smells too. Timothy's sharp nose caught the scent of birds and beetles and lots of interesting things. This was one of the most thrilling places he had ever set his paws in!

'Over here, Timmy,' called George as she pulled out a trunk full of old toys that had belonged to her when she was a lot smaller.

She opened the lid and looked inside. There were some old toy cars and a train set she hadn't played with for ages. There were some picture books too and several old jigsaw puzzles and a box full of wooden building bricks.

'Oh, Timmy, here's my old football!' she cried, holding up a rather sorry-looking leather ball that was flat as a pancake. 'I remember it got a puncture and Father was too busy to ever mend it.'

'Wuff,' said Timothy, thinking that a flat old football wouldn't be much good for a proper game.

George brought out something else and held it up. 'And here's my cowboy outfit that I grew out of. I'm sure some little boy will be pleased to buy it at the sale.' She put it to one side to take down to her mother.

Then George came across a cardboard box and opened it. Inside was a doll with blonde hair and dressed in a pink satin frock. 'Ugh!' she cried, screwing up her nose. 'This can go to the jumble sale, Timmy, that's for sure!'

The doll had been sent to George one Christmas by an aunt and uncle who lived in London. The aunt and uncle had three children who were George's cousins. Their names were Julian, Dick and

Anne. George had never met them and did not particularly want to. Especially as one of them was a girl!

'My cousin Anne probably likes dolls and Aunt must have thought I liked them too,' said George to Timothy, who was staring at the doll as if he would like to grab it and shake it hard between his sharp little teeth. 'That just shows what she knows about *me*!' she added haughtily, putting the doll on top of the cowboy outfit.

'Wuff,' said Timothy, agreeing as usual.

Soon there was quite a pile of things for the sale. George looked around for something to put them in. She spotted a large, empty cardboard box and went to fetch it. In the bottom was a scrap of old newspaper, tattered and yellow and rather cobwebby. A word written on the torn headline caught her sharp eyes.

'Detectives Hunt for Bones,' she read out loud to Timothy. 'A search is taking place in Kirrin Bay for . . .' she stopped and gave a sigh. 'The rest of the story is missing,' she said, turning to the puppy with a sparkle in her vivid blue eyes. 'Detectives in Kirrin Bay, though. How exciting, Timmy!'

She turned over the ragged piece of newspaper but there was only an advertisement on the other side. The date was years and years ago.

'Oh, well,' said the little girl. 'I suppose we'll never know the rest of the story.' She screwed up the paper and threw it away. 'Come on,

Timmy. Let's get this stuff down to Mummy, then we can go out for a walk.'

'Wuff,' said Timothy excitedly. '*Walk*' was another word he knew very well indeed!

When George showed her mother the box of toys, she was very pleased. 'I'm sure the organizers will be delighted,' she said. 'Thank you, George. It's such a lovely day, why don't you take Timmy out along the beach?'

'All right, Mummy,' said George. Then she had an exciting idea. 'I know, Timmy, let's have a picnic!'

'Wuff,' said Timothy, his big ears pricking upright. He loved picnics. Joanna, the woman who cooked for the family and helped George's mother in the house, made wonderful cakes and pies. If he was very good he might be allowed to have some. A picnic sounded a marvellous idea.

'Go into the kitchen and ask Joanna to make you some sandwiches,' said George's mother.

'Come on, Tim,' said George. 'We'll go for a swim too if you like.'

'Wuff,' barked Timothy joyfully. If there was one thing he liked beside walks, bones and picnics, it was splashing around in the warm waters of Kirrin Bay.

In the kitchen, Joanna was making a batch of bread. It smelled delicious and George's mouth watered as she ran in with Timothy at her heels.

'Mmm, Joanna!' she exclaimed, eyeing two warm freshly baked loaves on the kitchen table. 'Could you make me some sandwiches with that lovely bread? Timmy and I are going to have a picnic.'

'A picnic? Oh, well, I should think so,' said Joanna with a smile. She was a round woman with a jolly face. 'What else would you like to go with them?' The pantry at Kirrin Cottage was always full of delicious things to make picnics with.

'Oh, some of your luscious apple pie and homemade lemonade,' cried George. 'And some cheese, and some of Mummy's ripe tomatoes to go with the bread, please . . . ooh, and some plums from the garden too.'

'Right you are,' said Joanna, laughing and bustling about getting the picnic ready.

'And please may Timmy have some of his biscuits and a bone?' called George over her shoulder as she ran upstairs to get her swimming costume and a towel.

Soon the picnic was ready. Joanna had packed it in George's rucksack. George stuffed her swimming things in too and hitched it up on her back. She ran outside into the fresh air. Timothy scampered after her, his tail waving in the air like a banner. He had sniffed all the goodies going into the rucksack and couldn't wait for picnic time. This was going to be tremendous fun!

3

Timothy goes digging

Down the garden the little girl and her puppy went on their way to the beach. Skipping past the old apple tree where George had built a tree-house high up in the branches. Past the garden shed and Mother's flower-beds and vegetable patch. And through the gate that led to the cliff path.

The path led down to the bay. Down they went, Timothy scampering on ahead sniffing for rabbits and birds and anything else interesting that might have passed that way.

George stuck her hands in the pockets of her jeans. She whistled a merry tune and thought how lucky she was to live so close to the sea and have such a lovely friend as Timothy to play with.

It was a lovely sunny day as the two ran down the path to the shore. White fluffy clouds drifted across a blue sky and the air was full of birdsong and the buzzing of insects in the heather.

Kirrin Bay was a wide, curved stretch of golden sand, shining in the bright sunlight. Little waves broke on the shore with hardly a murmur. A flock of seagulls wheeled and dived in the clear air. George took a deep breath. She loved the bay and the island. They really were the best places in the whole wide world.

They soon found a good place in the shelter of a large rock to have their picnic. George shrugged off her rucksack and quickly made a hollow in the warm sand. She sat down inside it, staring out at Kirrin Island. She felt the sun warming her skin and smelled the wonderful scent of the sea.

Timothy sat beside her for a minute or two. Then he jumped up and rushed, barking, down the beach chasing a flock of seagulls that had landed close to the water's edge.

'Don't chase the birds, Timothy!' shouted George sternly. 'You know I've told you that before!' She loved all the seabirds and didn't want Timothy scaring them away.

The puppy came back to her looking rather sorry for himself. He *knew* he wasn't allowed to chase them. Somehow, though, he just couldn't help it. He didn't really know what his dear mistress was worried about. He never, ever caught one. In fact, he became very annoyed when they flew off out of his reach. How was a puppy supposed to catch things that flew so high in the air?

George grinned at him and gave him a hug. 'Sorry, darling Tim, but you know you mustn't do it,' she said.

'Wurf,' Timothy said, as if to apologize.

'Sit down here, there's a good boy,' said George, patting the sand beside her. 'It's so lovely and warm.'

When Timothy was sitting down beside her, she unpacked her rucksack. She took out the packet of sandwiches and opened one up. Joanna had put cheese and pickle inside. Her very favourite, especially if eaten with home-grown tomatoes. She gave Timothy a handful of biscuits. The puppy soon crunched and chewed his way through them and watched George enviously as she munched away at her sandwiches. Joanna's bread tasted as delicious as it had smelled.

When George had finished the sandwiches she gave Timothy a piece of crust, then ate her slice of apple pie. She washed it down with a swig of lemonade straight from the bottle. It tasted much better that way. She rounded off her feast with two juicy red plums from the garden, then tried to see how far she could spit the stones.

One of the stones went right to the water's edge.

'Brilliant, don't you think, Timmy?' laughed George. 'I bet I can spit further than any boy in the world.'

'Wurf,' agreed Timothy, even though he thought spitting stones seemed to be rather a silly thing to do. Chasing gulls was much more fun.

'Mmm, Timmy, I'm really full up,' said the little girl, giving a sigh of contentment.

She lay down in her sand hollow with her face up to the sun. Timothy lay beside her, his head between his paws, staring longingly at the seagulls.

'We'll go for a swim when our picnic has gone down,' said George, knowing it was not wise to swim directly after eating. 'Then we'll have a lovely splash about.'

Half an hour later, she jumped up. 'I'm going for a swim now, Timmy,' she said. 'Coming?' She quickly stripped off her jeans and shirt and put on her costume. Timothy barked with excitement and ran with her to the edge of the water. George dived in. She was a very fast, very strong swimmer for a little girl of her age and could hold her breath underwater for ages.

Timothy was still too little to swim so he paddled and splashed about close to the edge for a while then came out and sat waiting patiently for George as she swum strongly up and down like a little seal.

Something caught the puppy's eye and he wandered off away from the edge of the waves. He sniffed around behind one of the rocks. It was a very tall pointed rock called Needle Rock. His plumy tail wagged with excitement. There was a very interesting smell here that he had not come across before!

By the time George came out of the water Timothy had dug quite a deep hole for such a small puppy. George shook the water from her eyes and ran to get her clothes. As she quickly dressed, she noticed Timothy's rear end sticking out of the hole, his tail waving like a flag.

'Timmy! What *are* you up to?' she laughed, running over to see what was going on.

Timothy came out backwards and shook a whole shower of sand out of his shaggy coat. She saw he had something in his mouth.

'What *have* you found?' cried the little girl in amazement, for, lying in front of Timothy, was a large bone. It was long and thick and had strange-looking knobs at one end although the other end was broken and jagged.

George gave a gasp of surprise. She picked up the bone and stared at it. 'Timmy!' she exclaimed. 'Fancy finding a bone buried in Kirrin Bay. However did it get here?'

Then she suddenly remembered the torn piece of newspaper she had found in the loft back at Kirrin Cottage. *Detectives Search for Bones*! She looked at Timothy excitedly. 'Oh, Timmy,' she cried. 'Have we found one of the bones the detectives were searching for, do you think?'

'Wuff,' said Timothy, wondering how long it would be before his small mistress gave him back his bone so he could start chewing it.

'I think we'd better take it home straightaway,' said George. 'I don't know *what* Mummy and Father are going to say when they see it!'

4

Father's strange reaction

'What on earth have you got there?' exclaimed George's mother as they came through the gate and into the garden with the bone Timothy had dug from the sand.

George was quite red in the face from hurrying back up the cliff path to the cottage.

'A bone,' said George, pulling it out of her rucksack. It had been sticking out of the top as it was far too long to fit inside.

'That's odd,' said Mother, gazing at it with a frown on her face. 'Where did you find it?'

'Timmy dug it up on the beach near Needle Rock,' explained George. She went close to her mother and gazed up at her. 'Do you think it's a *human* bone?' she said in a low voice.

'Oh, I don't think so, darling,' laughed her mother kindly. 'What would a human bone be doing buried in our dear Kirrin Bay?'

'Well, I—' began George but she was interrupted by her father coming out of the back door looking for his wife.

'Fanny!' called the tall man. 'What time does the train go again?'

'Father's going up to London,' explained Mother. 'I'd better go and write down the train times otherwise he'll probably forget them altogether.' She handed the bone back to George and hurried indoors.

George and Timothy followed her. Father had gone back to his study. He had forgotten to wait for his wife to tell him what time the train left.

'I'm going to show him the bone, Timmy,' said George, hurrying after him. 'He'll know all about it, I'm sure!' She ran along the hall and knocked on the study door.

'Who is it?' came an irritable voice from inside. 'I'm busy.'

'You can't be busy, Father,' said George, opening the door and going in. 'You're supposed to be going to catch the train to London.'

'Am I?' said Father, looking up from his notebook. George could see the pages were covered with very important formulas. 'Oh yes, of course I am.' George's father was very absent-minded and often forgot things. He shut the book with a bang and put it in his briefcase. 'What did you want, George? I've got to go in a minute.'

George held up the bone. 'Do you know what kind of a bone this is, Father?' Timothy tried to jump up and grab it. 'Down!' she commanded sternly.

Timothy sat down looking rather hurt. After all it was *his* bone. He had been the one to dig it up.

George's father stared very hard at the bone, then took it from her. 'Where on earth did you find this, George?' he asked, frowning deeply.

'Timmy dug it up on the beach,' answered the little girl. 'Don't you think it's strange, Father?'

'Very,' said Father, suddenly sounding very excited. He stroked his chin, his dark eyes gleaming. 'Very strange and rather marvellous, I think. I'll take it up to London with me and show it to a friend of mine. My word, George, I've got a feeling this bone could be very important! Very important indeed!'

Then George's father did something very unusual. He bent down and gave Timothy a hug and a pat. 'Well *done*, Timmy! Good boy!' he exclaimed.

'Don't you think you should tell the police?' asked George, feeling rather puzzled at her father's strange behaviour.

Father stared at her. 'Police? Don't be silly, George,' he said. 'This bone is far too old for them to be interested in.'

'But—' she began. But she didn't get any further as her father picked up his briefcase, pushed past and hurried out of the room.

The two followed. Father took his coat and hat from the hallstand and opened the front door. 'Goodbye, Fanny,' he called.

'I'll see you tomorrow.'

The last George saw of him was as he walked briskly out of the front gate and down the road towards the railway station. Mother ran after him and gave him the train times she had written down. He stuffed the piece of paper into his pocket, kissed her quickly, then hurried off again. He looked most peculiar with a large bone in one hand and his briefcase in the other.

Mother came back to the house looking puzzled. 'Why has Quentin taken that bone with him?' she asked George.

'I've no idea,' said George, feeling annoyed. 'It was Timmy's bone and he just took it away without even asking permission.'

'But what is he going to *do* with it?' asked her mother, still looking rather puzzled.

'He said he's going to show it to a friend of his,' said George.

'Oh, well, never mind, dear,' said Mother, patting George's dark curls. 'I'm sure Father knows what he's doing.'

'I hope so,' said George with a sigh. She bent to give Timmy a hug. 'Sorry, Tim, it looks as if you've lost your bone for now.'

What could have been an exciting and mysterious adventure had turned out to be rather a damp squib after all.

George and Timothy wandered out into the garden. George stood under the apple tree gazing up at her tree-house. She had been racking her brains for a way to get Timothy up there. Joanna's husband William, who sometimes helped Mother in the garden, had made a ladder but she couldn't climb up carrying the dog. She did try once but he wriggled and she was afraid she might drop him.

Timothy sat and stared at the tree-house too. He was longing to get up there and explore for any exciting smells.

'Wuff,' he said sadly.

George bent down and gave him another hug. 'Never mind, Tim, we'll think of a way of getting you up there, don't worry.'

When she went indoors Mother was standing in the hall with Father's small suitcase in her hand.

'Your father's forgotten to take his night things,' she said with a sigh. 'One day he'll forget his own head.'

George giggled at the thought of her father running for the train with a bone and a brief-case but no head!

That evening there was a telephone call from him. George was reading her adventure comic in the lounge when the phone rang.

'Very well, Quentin,' she heard her mother say. 'I'll get the spare rooms ready. About midday? Yes, very well. Goodbye, dear.'

George's mother put the phone down and came into the lounge. 'We're having visitors, George,' she said. 'They're coming with Father tomorrow.'

'Visitors!' exclaimed George, looking up from her comic. 'Oh, blow! I hate visitors!'

'Well, that's too bad, dear,' said her mother. 'Your father's bringing his friend back from London to stay for a few days, so I hope you'll be polite and not scowl at him all the time.'

'What is he coming here for?' asked George curiously.

'He's very excited about that bone you found and he wants you to show him exactly where Timmy dug it up,' said her mother.

'The tide will have washed away the hole,' said George. 'But I suppose we can still find the place, if we have to, can't we, Tim, darling?'

'Wuff,' said Timothy. He was rather puzzled about all the fuss being made about a bone. He had always thought it was *dogs* who became excited about bones, not humans!

5

Visitors!

'Who *is* Father's friend?' asked George curiously when her mother announced they were to have visitors. 'Is he a detective?' She thought perhaps a policeman was coming to find out about the bone Timothy had dug out of the sand.

'Don't be silly, dear,' said her mother. 'Your father's friends are all scientists, like him.'

That was twice people had told George not to be silly when she'd mentioned policemen. She thought she had better not mention them again. She hated grown-ups telling her she was being silly when most of the time it was *them* who were being silly.

'Father's friend is a palaeontologist,' explained her mother.

'A *what?*' asked George, who was not very good at knowing what long words meant.

'He studies old bones and fossils,' said her mother patiently. 'He's a sort of bone professor.'

George screwed up her nose. Studying bones seemed a very peculiar thing to do. Unless you were a dog, of course.

'Does he want to study the bone Timmy found, then?' asked George.

'Apparently,' said her mother. 'And he also wants to see if he can find any more like it. Oh, and by the way he's bringing his son with him.'

'His son!' exclaimed George.

'Yes,' said her mother. 'So I want you to be nice to him, George. They live in the city and aren't used to life in the country so you'll have to be very patient and kind.'

'Patient and kind!' exclaimed George. 'Is he a baby, then?' She felt very angry and upset. She really didn't want any city boy staying at Kirrin Cottage. She and Timmy were having such a lovely time. A city boy would spoil everything!

'No, of course he isn't. He's about your age, I believe,' said Mother. 'It'll be nice for you to have someone to play with.'

'I've *got* someone to play with,' said George, flinging down her comic. 'I've got Timmy and I don't want anyone else, thank you very much, Mummy!'

She stormed out of the room, with Timmy scampering behind her. He didn't know why his little mistress was so upset.

After all, the visitor *could* have been a girl. George would have hated *that* even more!

George strode through the kitchen and out of the back door, slamming it hard behind her. She went to her garden swing and sat on it, moodily swinging to and fro. Trust Father to ruin the holidays for her. She would have to be friendly and polite to people she didn't even know. It was just too bad!

Father and the visitors arrived at noon the following day. Joanna had been busy since very early morning making cakes and pies for them, washing lettuces and tomatoes from the garden and baking a huge batch of fresh bread.

'Boys have enormous appetites,' she said when George was giving Timothy his breakfast.

'So have girls,' said George indignantly. 'Especially ones like me!'

'That's true,' said Joanna, smiling broadly at the little tomboy.

George's mother was bustling about, going up and down the stairs with armfuls of clean sheets and blankets. George decided to keep out of the way, so she took Timothy for a very long walk on the moor. She was still angry at the thought of having a stranger to stay. She had always been on her own and had grown rather selfish. She loved sharing things with Timothy but sharing with another person was different altogether.

It was cool and drizzly that morning as George and Timothy set off. Grey clouds loomed overhead and the bushes were festooned with raindrops.

Timothy scampered on ahead, his shaggy coat picking up drops of rain as he ran along.

Up the narrow path they went, between wild strips of scratchy heather. This was the place where George had found Timothy, crouching in the undergrowth, alone and scared.

Today though, the puppy was with his beloved mistress and he trotted along happily, sniffing for rabbits and hedgehogs.

George walked with her head down, muttering to herself and kicking at the stones with the toe of her Wellington boot. 'Visitors! That's spoiled all our adventures now, Timmy, you wait and see.'

She put Timothy on his lead and went as close to the cliff edge as she dared. On the horizon the sun was peeping through the clouds and sending bright pathways down to the sea. Behind them, the drizzly sky was rolling away. It was going to be a lovely day after all.

George sat down, not minding about the damp grass. Timothy lay down beside her and rested his head on her lap. 'Oh, well, Tim,' she said with a sigh. 'The sun's going to come out after all. I suppose it won't be *too* bad having the bone professor to stay. And I suppose it *might* be fun having a boy to make friends with.'

Timothy gave a little whine and wagged his tail very hard. He gazed up at George from under his shaggy eyebrows. 'Wuff,' he said and licked her hand. He was pleased his mistress was feeling more cheerful.

'Darling Tim!' said George, laughing and giving him a hug. 'I knew you'd agree!' She got to her feet, suddenly feeling a lot better. 'Come on, let's get home.'

Safely away from the cliff edge, George let the puppy off his lead again. He bounced on ahead, running back the way they had come. The sun had come out now and steam rose from the damp ground.

The sea sparkled and the sky was a vivid blue. It really was too nice to be miserable.

When she arrived back at Kirrin Cottage, George saw at once that the visitors had arrived. Joanna was setting lunch out on the lawn and George could hear voices through the French windows. She stood in the doorway shuffling her feet.

'Georgina and Timmy will be back shortly and they'll show you round,' she heard her mother say.

'*Georgina!*' hissed George to Timothy, scowling fiercely. 'Why is she calling me *that?*'

Someone replied from the other side of the room. The person was hidden by the long curtains that framed the doorway.

'It's rather too hot to do *anything*,' the voice said in a kind of whining tone. 'I shan't want to go out in the sun, it's awfully bad for you, you know.'

'I'm afraid Georgina plays outside all the time,' said Mother. 'She's as brown as a berry.'

'Perhaps Timmy will stay in with me, then,' said the voice. 'I don't know much about girls anyway, to be honest. There are only boys at my school, you see.'

George giggled. The bone professor's son thought Timmy was a *boy*! What fun!

'Will you be helping your father dig for the bones, Jack?' asked George's father, not bothering to explain about Timothy, if he had indeed even noticed what the boy had said.

'Not if it's this hot,' came the cross voice again.

Goodness, thought George. That boy sounds as grumpy as I am sometimes!

The curtain must have twitched because Father called out. 'Is that you, George? For goodness' sake stop lurking out there and come in and meet our guests!'

6

Clever Timmy!

Reluctantly, George stepped into the room to meet the visitors.

Timmy ran in front of her, wagging his tail. He really was a very friendly little dog.

The bone professor was standing in front of the fireplace. He was short and fat with a large head. He wore a rather crumpled-looking suit with a bright red shirt underneath. George had never seen anyone wearing a shirt *quite* that colour before. He also wore a battered-looking straw hat tilted to one side. George didn't think he looked a bit like a professor!

The professor's son, Jack, was lolling in the armchair. He was short and rather fat too. He wore small, steel-rimmed spectacles and peered at George over the top of them like a shiny-faced owl.

'Hello, young lady,' boomed the bone professor. 'Come in, come in, let's have a look at you.'

'I'm not a young lady,' said George, scowling. This seemed to be a very bad start. Anyone who called George a young lady was in her bad books straightaway!

The bone professor, whose name was Professor Ward, gave a hearty laugh. 'Oh, well, whatever you are,' he said. 'Come in and tell me exactly where you found that marvellous bone your father brought to show me.'

'Timmy found it, not me,' said George, still scowling. She really couldn't understand quite what was so wonderful about an old bone. Mysterious, yes. But *marvellous*?

'Where is Timmy, then?' piped up Jack, hoping at least he would have someone to play with.

'He's there, silly,' said George, forgetting to scowl and grinning as Timothy ran across and tried to playfully grab the boy's trouser leg.

'Oh, he's a *dog*,' laughed Jack, his irritable expression disappearing like magic. 'I like dogs.' He bent down and gently pulled Timothy away. 'I thought Tim was your brother!' He stroked the puppy's shaggy coat and gave him a hug.

Timothy wagged his tail and licked Jack's shiny face. Everyone laughed except George. She hated Timothy being friends with anyone but herself. She ran over and picked him up.

'He's better than a brother,' she said. 'He's my best friend.'

'And he'll be my best friend too if he'll show me where he found that bone,' said the professor.

'Wuff, wuff,' said Timothy, struggling to get down. George put him on the floor. He ran to the professor and sat at his feet, looking up and wagging his tail like mad.

'Wurf,' he barked excitedly and everyone laughed again. Except George. She was still scowling. If Timothy was going to like the bone professor and his son better than he liked her, having visitors was going to be worse than she'd thought!

George needn't have worried, though. The friendly puppy soon came back to her and sat by her feet, staring up at her with his big, melting brown eyes. He was only being polite to the visitors. He could never love anyone as much as he loved his small mistress.

Joanna had spread the table with a delicious salad. Fresh lettuce and tomatoes from the garden with smoked ham and potato salad, crisp spring onions and scarlet beetroot. She had baked a plum pie for pudding and made a large jug of creamy custard to go with it. Jack tucked in as if he had not eaten for a week. George could not help staring at him as he piled large helpings of everything on to his plate. Joanna was right about boys, she thought. They *did* have enormous appetites! She made up her mind there and then to try to eat just as much as he did.

'You see, young lady . . . er, Georgina . . .' began the professor when he had finished his salad.

'George,' said George, her mouth full of potato salad.

'She won't answer to Georgina,' whispered her mother in Professor Ward's ear.

'Oh . . . er . . . sorry,' said the professor. 'Well . . . George, then.'

'That's a boy's name,' said Jack, peering at her from over the top of his glasses and crunching a large mouthful of lettuce. This certainly was a strange family, he thought. A scientist who hardly ever came out of his study, a girl who looked like a boy, and a house in the middle of nowhere. Very strange indeed.

'That's why I like it,' said George, giving him one of her dark stares.

'George, are you going to listen to what the professor has to say?' asked her father sharply. 'Or are we going to spend all day discussing names?'

The professor leaned closer to George. 'George,' he said, smiling. 'The bone that Timmy found was very important indeed.'

'Yes, I know,' said George. 'I knew that detectives were looking for bones ages ago.'

'Detectives?' said Father with a frown. 'What are you talking about, George?'

George explained about the torn newspaper she had found in the loft.

Her father frowned and scratched his chin for a moment. 'I don't remember anything like that taking place,' he said, looking most puzzled.

'It must have been when the first old bone was found,' said his wife, laughing. 'Oh, George dear, no wonder you thought Father should tell the police. I remember the newspaper story now. It said *Dinosaur Detectives Hunt for Bones.*'

'I thought *detectives* meant policemen!' exclaimed George, feeling a bit silly.

Everyone laughed so loudly that George went red and scowled round at everybody. It wasn't *her* fault the newspaper had been torn and tattered.

'Trust a *girl* to think that,' said Jack scornfully, laughing louder than anyone.

George gave him one of her extra special glares. He really was horrible. How was she going to bear him staying at Kirrin Cottage? Worse still, when Jack laughed, Timmy ran over to him and jumped up, barking excitedly. Jack made a great fuss of him and, much to George's annoyance, Timothy seemed to like him very much.

'Come *here*, Timothy!' she called sternly. 'Now stay here,' she insisted as the puppy trotted back to her side. He sat down and looked up at her. He couldn't understand why she was angry with him. He was only being friendly.

'An easy mistake to make,' said Professor Ward kindly about George's misunderstanding. 'Now, George, let me explain. Several years ago someone found a fragment of dinosaur bone on the beach in Kirrin Bay.'

Dinosaurs! The scowl disappeared from George's face. Things were suddenly becoming *much* more interesting. Prehistoric animals were very thrilling indeed. 'I didn't know anything about that!' she exclaimed.

'It was before you were born,' explained her mother gently.

'There was great excitement,' continued the professor. 'Because the bone belonged to a type of prehistoric animal that was completely unknown to science.'

'Golly!' exclaimed George. 'Kirrin Bay must have been jolly famous then.'

'Yes, it was for a while,' said her mother. 'But although lots of people came here to search, no more bones were ever found.'

'Until Timothy found one,' added Father.

'Well,' said George, giving the puppy a hug. 'He *is* the cleverest dog in the world, you know.'

'Yes, I can see that,' said the bone professor with a smile. 'And I'm hoping that we can now find the whole skeleton. Wouldn't that be thrilling?'

'Yes,' said George thoughtfully. 'But it would be horrid if you dug up the whole of Kirrin Bay.'

'Oh, no, I promise you we won't do that,' said the professor, smiling again. 'If I think the site is interesting I'll get a team together to recover the rest of the bones. When we've finished I promise you your lovely bay will look just the same as it ever did.'

'Good,' said George.

When they had all finished eating, the professor stood up. 'Now,' he said eagerly. 'Shall we all go down to the bay?'

7

More bones

'I'm not coming,' said Jack, when his father suggested they all went down to the beach. 'I'll stay here with Timmy. I can't think of anything worse than tramping along a hot beach in the hot sunshine.'

'Oh, no, you won't,' said George, giving the boy another black look. 'Timmy comes everywhere with me!'

'I think you should let him stay just for once,' said her mother hastily. 'After all, Jack *is* our guest.'

'I don't care,' said George defiantly, calling Timothy and going out into the garden. 'He's not staying here! If Jack wants to play with him he'll have to come with the rest of us.'

She didn't really *want* the boy to go with them but she certainly wasn't leaving Timothy behind!

Jack gave a sigh and got up out of the chair. 'Oh, all right,' he said, following her out. 'But if the heat makes me ill, it'll be your fault.'

'Ill!' snorted George. She had thought girls were weak and babyish. Now it was jolly obvious that some boys were too!

Father gave a sigh as he came out with the professor. 'I'm afraid my daughter can be rather rude at times,' he said.

If anyone tries to take Timmy away from me, thought George, I can be a lot ruder than that!

So down to Kirrin Bay everyone went on a bone hunt. Father, Mother and the professor, the edges of his jacket flapping in the breeze and his hat tilted jauntily to one side.

George ran on ahead with Timothy bounding by her side. 'Dinosaurs, Timmy!' said the little girl excitedly to her puppy friend. 'They're enormous! Can you imagine them living at Kirrin Bay?'

Timothy barked as if to say, 'I wouldn't care *how* big they were. I'd bark and bark until they ran away!'

Last of all came Jack. He squinted in the bright sun and lagged behind. He looked very hot and bothered indeed as they crossed the sand towards the place where Timothy had found the dinosaur bone. George could see that the walk to the shore had been worse than Jack had imagined. She supposed it must be very difficult to walk on the sand when you had only been used to hard pavements. The sun was beating down on his head like a hot iron and he looked completely out of breath already.

'Who does that island belong to?' panted the boy when he caught up with the others.

'Me,' replied George.

'Don't be silly.' Jack screwed up his eyes as he stared out towards Kirrin Island. 'How can a girl own an island?'

'Well, it's *almost* mine,' said George. 'It belongs to Mummy and she's promised to give it to me one day. And the castle too!'

'A likely story,' Jack said disbelievingly, going to sit in the shade of one of the big rocks. 'I'm staying here.' He flopped down with a sigh and wiped his face with his handkerchief.

'I don't care if you don't believe me. It's true, so there!' said George indignantly, running on ahead to catch up with the others.

They all stopped close to Needle Rock. 'Now, George,' said

Professor Ward. 'Can you show me exactly where the little fellow found it?'

'Show them, Timmy,' said George and the puppy ran round the rock. Straightaway he began digging again. Showers of sand and shingle flew up into the air.

The professor followed and caught hold of the puppy's collar, hauling him gently away. 'Good boy!' he said. 'Good boy, Timmy!'

Timothy's tail wagged nineteen to the dozen. This was excellent fun but rather puzzling. If he dug holes in the garden he was told off. Now someone was *praising* him for digging. What funny things humans were!

George held him back while the professor knelt down and examined the hole closely. He didn't seem to notice that the knees of his trousers were getting damp and sandy. He picked something up and took a magnifying glass from his pocket, peering at it closely.

Everyone held their breath. Had the professor found another fragment of bone?

At last the professor put down the glass and beamed up at all of them. 'This is definitely a piece of very ancient bone indeed,' he said excitedly. 'The tides must have washed away many layers of sand and left the skeleton close to the surface.' He stood up with a broad smile on his kindly face. 'I think we've made a find, Quentin! I need to get up to London and get a team organized right away.'

Everyone trooped back to Kirrin Cottage and Professor Ward went into Father's study to make some important telephone calls.

'We're not going to have all the other diggers staying here as well, are we, Mummy?' asked George in horror.

'No, of course not,' said her mother. 'They'll stay at a hotel in the nearest town.'

'That's good,' said George with a sigh of relief.

'Why don't you take Jack to see your tree-house?' said Mother, while they were waiting for the professor to finish his calls. 'I'm sure Father and Professor Ward will be in the study for hours discussing ideas.'

'Oh, all right,' said George, looking round for Jack. But the boy was nowhere to be seen. He had tramped back to Kirrin Cottage with everyone, then disappeared.

'I saw him go outside and into the garden shed,' said Joanna.

'The shed?' exclaimed George. 'What on earth is he doing in there?'

'I've no idea,' said Joanna from where she was standing with a big pile of ironing.

'Go and see, there's a good girl,' said George's mother. 'I'm sure he'll be glad of your company.'

'I don't know why you think that, Mummy,' said George. 'He

doesn't like me one little bit.'

'Well, go anyway,' insisted her mother patiently. 'Show him your tree-house. He's bound to like it . . . and be nice to him!' she added.

'Very well,' said George scowling. 'Come on, Timmy.'

Down the garden path the two went. The potting shed door was open and inside, Jack was fiddling around with something.

'What are you doing?' asked George curiously, standing in the doorway, watching.

Jack turned round, looking rather guilty. 'Nothing,' he said.

'Yes, you are,' insisted George, going in and seeing the boy had been examining an old clock her mother had put out for the jumble sale. 'That's my mother's clock, you know.'

'It's broken,' said Jack.

'We know that, silly,' said George 'That's why it's going to the jumble sale.'

'I could mend it,' said Jack. 'I'm awfully good at mending things.'

'You can if you like,' said George, shrugging. 'But I'm supposed to be showing you my tree-house.'

'Tree-house?' said Jack, pulling a face. 'Oh . . . I don't like things like that.' He opened the back of the clock and peered inside. 'I'm scared of heights.'

George gave an irritated sigh. Jack was a very peculiar boy indeed. How could anyone *not* like tree-houses?

8

A secret

'I suppose you don't like swimming or sailing either, then,' said George scornfully when Jack told her he didn't like tree-houses.

'No,' said Jack, poking a small screwdriver into the back of the old clock he had been examining. 'I hate them. I like reading and making and mending things.'

'Well, please yourself,' said George, going out and leaving Jack to his own devices.

George fetched Timothy's ball and took him down the garden to play. He had become very good at fetching a ball and soon brought it back when she threw it as far as she could. He barked excitedly and ran round in circles waiting for her to throw it again. He never seemed to get tired of the game.

'Can I have a go?' asked a voice behind her ten minutes later.

George turned round. Jack was standing there. 'I thought you were mending the clock,' said George.

'I've done it,' said Jack.

George stared at him, screwing up her nose. 'You can't have,' she said. 'It's been broken for ages. How could you mend it so quickly?'

'I told you I was good at mending things,' said Jack. 'I've taken it indoors and put it on the kitchen table.'

'Oh,' said George, rather taken aback. Jack might be a strange kind of boy but it looked as if he was awfully clever all the same.

Reluctantly she let Jack throw the ball for Timothy two or three times. Jack enjoyed the game. He seemed to have quite forgotten that being out in the sun was bad for him.

'You'd better look at the tree-house or Mummy will think I haven't let you see it,' said George, annoyed because Timothy was enjoying his game with the boy.

'All right, then,' said Jack, sighing as if tree-houses were the most boring things in the world instead of one of the best.

George stood underneath the tall old apple tree and pointed upwards. 'Up there,' she said. 'I made most of it myself although William, Joanna's husband, gave me that big wooden box.' The box was nailed to several wooden boards. George had heaved the boards up into the tree and nailed them to a thick branch. The house was rather ramshackle but George thought it was great fun. The only thing that spoiled it was that Timothy was unable to play up there with her. He just sat underneath and whined all the time.

George went to get the ladder from behind the tree. 'Do you want to go up?' she asked.

'Not likely,' said Jack. 'It looks a bit of a shambles to me,' he added, staring at the house. 'If you had a strong gale it would blow down.'

'No, it wouldn't. We've had lots of gales and it's still there,' said George indignantly.

How dare he be rude about her wonderful tree-house! She was very proud of it. She didn't care that it was a bit lopsided and ramshackle. It was still the best tree-house in the world.

'What does Timmy think of it?' asked Jack.

'He doesn't think anything,' admitted George. 'I can't get him up there.'

Jack made a face and turned away. It was obvious he didn't think much of the tree-house at all. For one thing it was much too high up. For another it looked as if it might collapse at any minute. If you were going to build something, thought Jack, you should jolly well do it properly.

George's mother came out of the back door and through the garden to find them. 'George, dear,' she said. 'Was it you who put that old clock in the kitchen?'

'No,' said George, pointing rather rudely at Jack. 'It was *him*. He's mended it.' Although she didn't like the boy she was very fair and honest and always told the truth.

Her mother turned to Jack. 'Jack! It's going again, ticking away merrily as if it had never stopped. You're a wonder.'

'Thanks,' said Jack. 'I'm good at things like that.'

George's mother smiled broadly and gave the boy a quick hug. 'Oh, Jack, that's marvellous! I'm very fond of the old clock but I really thought it would never go again. Thank you very much.'

Jack went bright red and looked down at his feet. 'That's all right,' he mumbled.

George wasn't very pleased that her mother had hugged Jack. She didn't like her mother being fond of him any more than she liked Timothy being his friend.

Just then they heard Professor Ward's voice calling them from the house and George's mother hurried back indoors to see what he wanted.

George and Jack followed more slowly. Half-way indoors Jack bent and picked Timothy up. 'I wish I had a dog for a friend,' he said wistfully. 'I've always wanted one but we live in a flat and there's nowhere for a dog to run and play.'

George quickly took Timothy from his arms. 'Well, you're not having mine,' she said haughtily and hurried on ahead.

* * *

When tea-time came, Joanna laid out fresh egg and cress sandwiches, a bowl of fresh strawberries, a jug of cream, a huge ginger cake and some chocolate biscuits on a small table by the French windows.

'Ah, Jack,' said the professor as he and George's mother came in for tea. 'I hear you've mended Fanny's clock.'

'It was easy,' said Jack, lolling in the chair.

'He's very clever with his hands,' said the professor. 'He's always inventing things.'

'Inventing things? Well, then, Jack,' said George's mother. 'I've got a little task for you.'

'What kind of a task?' asked Jack, sitting up and taking notice.

'Well, the birds are eating the tops of my vegetables,' she explained. 'I've hung all sorts of things round my vegetable patch but they take no notice. No notice at all.'

'Oh,' said Jack. 'Do you want me to invent something that will scare them away, then?'

'Oh, yes please,' exclaimed George's mother. 'It would be lovely if you could.'

'I'm sure I'll be able to,' said Jack, helping himself to two sandwiches. He looked pleased George's mother had asked him. At least it would stop him being bored.

George felt furious. How dare her mother ask this boy to make a bird scarer! *She* was as good as any boy. *She* could easily have made one. She glared at her mother. But her mother was used to such scowls from her short-tempered daughter and ignored her.

'You can do it while I'm in London,' said Professor Ward. 'I'm going to recruit my team and I've invited Fanny and Quentin to come and stay with your mother and I for the night so we can go on an outing to the theatre.'

'I haven't got to go with you, have I?' asked George, hating the thought of all that traffic and noise and no views of the sea and the moors from the windows of their flat.

'No, dear,' said her mother. 'You're going to stay here with Jack.

Joanna is going to look after you both.'

'With Jack?' said George, sounding horrified.

'Yes,' said the professor. 'It'll do him good to spend some time by the sea.'

'Does he have to stay, Mummy?' asked George rather rudely. 'Timmy and I will be perfectly all right on our own.'

Timothy barked and went over to Jack as he held out a crust from his sandwich. The puppy wolfed it down then begged for another piece.

George scowled and took a large bite of ginger cake. But even *that* didn't make her feel better! The thought of Jack staying at Kirrin Cottage was really too much to bear!

George's mother sighed. 'George, it really will be nice for you to have Jack here!'

'Yes, Mummy,' said George, still in a huff.

'Wuff,' said Timothy, then lay down as George frowned at him. He stared at her with his head between his shaggy front paws. He quite liked this Jack boy. Especially as he had given him almost a whole sandwich.

'Do I have to stay, Dad?' asked Jack. He obviously didn't like the thought of staying at Kirrin Cottage much either.

'Yes, certainly, you do,' said his father, the professor. 'It will be good for you to get some fresh, country air for a change.'

'You can go swimming and sailing with George,' said her mother. 'And I'm sure she'll row you across to the island.'

'He doesn't like the sea,' said George sulkily.

'Now there's something very important I must tell both of you before I go,' said the professor. 'I'd like you both to keep our discovery a secret. If anyone finds out, we could have hordes of people down here looking for more bones.'

'We won't tell anyone,' promised George. 'Will we, Jack?'

'No,' mumbled Jack, still looking fed up.

'And also,' continued his father, 'rival professors would dearly like to get their hands on the skeleton. It's an unknown species and it'll be very valuable. So please don't mention it to anyone.'

George felt rather thrilled at this cloak and dagger kind of secret. 'Do you hear that, Timmy?' she whispered in the puppy's ear. 'We *love* keeping secrets, don't we?'

'Wurf,' said Timothy softly. 'Wurf, wurf!'

9

Jack makes a mistake

The following day dawned bright and sunny. George's father and mother and Professor Ward caught the early morning train to London, leaving George and Jack in Joanna's care. The kindly woman often stayed to look after George while her parents went away.

Joanna was in the kitchen cooking breakfast and humming merrily to herself as the little girl came down the stairs.

The delicious smell of bacon and eggs wafted from the frying pan. George couldn't help her mouth watering.

'Fresh country bacon and farm eggs,' said Joanna when Jack came through the door and she saw him eyeing the frying pan too. 'Not like those things you get in the city. No taste to them at all. Now, you two, what are you going to do with yourselves today?'

'I need to buy some things for the bird scarer,' replied Jack. 'Is there a shop in the village?'

'Oh, yes, dear,' said Joanna. 'Mrs Wood's post-office stores. She sells everything from tintacks to tinned tomatoes.'

'Thank you,' said Jack. 'I'll go after breakfast.'

'Are you going to show Jack how to get there?' Joanna asked George, placing a large plate of sizzling bacon and eggs in front of her.

'If he wants me to,' said George, tucking in.

'Can we catch the bus?' asked Jack.

'Don't be silly,' said George. 'We walk!'

'Walk?' said Jack, looking rather horrified. 'I hope it isn't far. It's jolly hot again today.'

'Of course it's not far,' said George scornfully. 'Timmy and I go there all the time, don't we, Tim? It's a lovely walk across the moor.'

'Wuff,' said Timothy, sitting at Jack's feet and gazing up at him hopefully. The smell of fried bacon really was the most delicious smell in the world.

'Oh well,' said Jack, pulling a face. 'If there isn't a bus I suppose we'll *have* to.'

After breakfast George, Timmy and Jack went along the path that led over the moor to the village. Jack puffed and panted as they ambled along. The sun blazed down from a wonderful blue sky and in the distance they could hear a skylark, its song rising and falling on the morning air.

George was striding on ahead with Timmy.

'Wait for me,' puffed Jack, stumbling a little. 'Phew,' he said as they waited for him to catch up. 'I'm not used to walking everywhere.'

By the time they reached the end of the path, Jack was very red in the face. George and Timothy hadn't slowed down at all and he was very relieved when they came to the gentle slope that led to the village.

George lagged behind a little. She hated shopping and would much rather play with Timothy and watch the fishing fleet sail out from the little harbour. 'You go on,' she said to Jack. 'I'm going to have a game with Timmy on the beach. Just carry on along the street and you'll soon come to the shop.'

'Righty-ho,' said Jack, hurrying off.

George and Timothy ran along the harbour wall and jumped down on to the pebbles. George found an old shoe that had been washed up by the tide and soon they were having a grand game.

'Come on, Timmy,' George said a while later when they had finished their games and sat for a while watching the fishing fleet. 'We'd better go and see if Jack's finished his shopping.'

When they reached the post-office stores, George could see through the window that Jack had his arms full of all sorts of things. String, sheets of cardboard, glue, jars of poster paint, a roll of tin foil. George couldn't think what he was going to do with them.

As she went in, Jack was talking to a tall, scruffy-looking boy of about fifteen. He was a stranger in the village.

'I live in London too,' said Jack.

'Are you on holiday here, then?' asked the boy.

'Oh, no, I'm here with my father. He's a professor, you know,' answered Jack, obviously trying to impress the older boy.

'A professor, eh?' remarked the youth, laughing in rather a rough way. 'What's he doing in a boring place like this, then?'

Boring? thought George angrily. How dare this horrid youth call Kirrin boring! It was the most beautiful place in the world.

She was just about to go and tell the boy what she thought of him when she heard Jack reply. 'Yes, it is rather, isn't it?' said Jack. 'But my father's found some extremely rare and valuable prehistoric bones down in the bay, you see.'

'Valuable?' said the youth, raising his thick, dark eyebrows in surprise.

'Yes,' said Jack, lowering his voice a little. 'They were behind a big pointed rock. He—'

But Jack didn't get any further. George marched up to him. She grabbed his arm angrily and pulled him away from the youth.

'For goodness' sake, Jack!' she hissed from between clenched teeth. 'You're not supposed to tell anyone, remember?' She dragged him to one side. Timothy barked excitedly, thinking they were playing a game of some sort.

'Be quiet, Timmy!' commanded George sternly and the little dog quietened down at once.

"That boy was bragging about his dad being a rich and important businessman so I thought I'd tell him about *my* father,' said Jack, shaking George's hand off.

'Well, you shouldn't have done,' said George, still feeling very angry indeed. 'Just wait until I tell your father that you've spoiled his secret!'

'Please don't tell my dad,' wailed Jack when he had paid for his things and they were outside. 'He'll be awfully angry. I'm sure that boy and his father wouldn't be interested in old bones.'

'I hope not, for your sake!' said George, striding off.

'Please . . .!' panted Jack, catching up with her. 'Please don't tell him. I'm terribly sorry.'

'All right, I won't tell your father,' said George, giving a sigh and calming down a little. 'But I won't be friends with someone who can't keep a secret!'

She strode off again at a fine old pace and Jack didn't catch up with her until they reached the gate of Kirrin Cottage. 'Come on, Timmy, let's go for a swim,' she said, so angry that she was determined not to speak to Jack again.

'Wuff,' said Timothy. A swim! What a lovely idea on such a hot and muggy day.

George didn't plan to see Jack for the rest of the day. She decided to ask Joanna to pack her and Timothy a picnic so they could spend the whole afternoon on the beach.

'Come on, Timmy,' she called when Joanna had got everything ready and she had fetched her swimming things from her room.

Timothy was outside exploring Mother's flower-beds. He poked his dear little black nose out from between the delphiniums when he heard his mistress calling him.

'Oh, Timmy!' cried George. 'Come out at once, Mummy will be so cross if you break her flowers!'

'Wuff,' said Timothy, coming out and standing in front of her with his pink tongue lolling out. Exploring flower-beds was hot work indeed. He sniffed the air. He could smell another picnic.

'Come on,' laughed George. 'At least you can't get up to mischief on the beach.'

Half-way along the garden path, George heard a clattering and banging sound. She turned round and saw the most peculiar sight. Jack had his head in the dustbin and was rummaging around in the rubbish. 'What *is* that boy doing now?' she asked Timothy in rather a puzzled voice.

Timothy gave a little whine as if to say he didn't have a clue.

'Oh well, I don't really care *what* he's doing,' said George with a shrug as they went through the gate. 'At least he doesn't want to come on our picnic. Thank goodness!'

Timothy bounded on ahead as George made her way along the narrow path to the beach. When Timothy came to the place where it sloped gently downwards he suddenly stopped and stared, his ears pricked up and his tail quivering.

'What's wrong, Tim?' called George, running to catch up.

A low growl came from Timothy's throat and she saw what he was staring at. Two people were walking along the beach, stopping now and then to pick up pieces of driftwood, examine them, then throw them into the sea.

'Oh, blow!' exclaimed George, her hand on Timothy's collar to stop him bounding off to bark at the strangers. 'I hate it when there are other people about. Let's wait until they've gone, shall we?'

'Wuff,' said Timothy, rather sorrowfully. He would have liked to run up to the people and bark until they went away so he and George could have the bay to themselves straightaway. He had smelled the delicious things Joanna had put in the picnic bag and his mouth was watering.

George sat down, hidden behind a tussock of grass and pulled Timothy down beside her.

It wasn't long before the two people began to make their way up the cliff path and disappeared out of sight.

'Thank goodness!' said George, heaving a sigh of relief. 'The coast's clear now, Timmy. Come on, race you to the sea!'

She jumped up and raced down the slope on to the sand. Timothy barked excitedly and bounced along beside her.

They spent the afternoon playing on the beach and eating the delicious picnic Joanna had made for them. George had a lovely swim while Timothy splashed about in the shallows, barking at the little wavelets and generally enjoying himself.

When they returned to Kirrin Cottage Jack was nowhere to be

seen but George heard noises coming from the garden shed and went to investigate.

Jack was in there, hammering and banging.

'He must be making Mummy's bird scarer,' said George, standing on tiptoe to try to peep in the window to see what he was doing. But the glass was too dirty to see through so she gave up and went on indoors.

Jack didn't come out of the shed until it was time for the evening meal. George was still too angry with him for betraying their secret to ask if he had finished the scarer, even though she was quite curious to see what it looked like.

That evening the fine, muggy weather gave way to a dark and thundery sky.

'There's going to be a storm,' said George, looking out of the window after they had eaten their evening meal.

Jack was lolling in the armchair reading one of George's father's science books. George preferred adventure stories and tales of pirates and smugglers and boys doing brave deeds. Her bookcase was full of them.

'A storm?' said Jack, looking faintly alarmed. 'How do you know?'

'The wind has swung round,' said George. 'And there are white horses in the bay.'

Jack stared out of the window at the sea. 'Where? I can't see any horses,' he said.

'It means the sea is choppy and the waves have got white tops on them, silly,' said George scornfully. 'I love storms, don't you?'

'No,' said Jack. 'I hate them.'

'Oh, you would!' said George. 'You're such a baby!'

'No, I'm not,' said Jack, going back to his book and not saying another word to her all the evening.

George went to bed early, leaving Jack still reading in the lounge. She put Timothy down on his blanket in the kitchen as usual.

'I'll come and get you later when Joanna has gone to bed,' she whispered in his ear.

George's father didn't allow dogs on beds so it was a tremendous secret that Timothy slept in George's room each night. George made sure she got up early each morning, slipped silently down the stairs and put Timothy back in the kitchen before anyone else was up so she never had to confess he had been in her room.

Timothy settled down, turning round and round to make himself a little nest while he waited for George to come back for him. Though he was a very brave puppy, he wasn't at all sure he liked the sound of a storm. The sooner he was up the stairs with George the better!

10

Storm!

It was late when the storm broke. Joanna and Jack had been in bed for ages and George had already tiptoed down and brought Timothy up from the kitchen.

The little girl and her dog sat on the bed watching the lightning flash through her small side window that overlooked the sea.

'Oh, Timmy!' said George, her heart thudding with excitement as the whole horizon was lit up. 'Isn't it thrilling!'

'Wurf,' said Timothy although he wasn't *quite* sure he really liked all the banging and crashing that was going on outside.

Rain lashed the eaves and the wind roared round the roof of the house. Gigantic waves were smashing on the shore in a tumble of white foam. George loved it. It sounded like a fierce battle going on, with swords clashing and horses' hooves thundering.

Each time the lightning burst across the dark sky, Kirrin Island and the castle were lit up for an instant. They looked more mysterious and exciting than ever.

Suddenly, in-between crashes, there was a knock at George's door.

'Oh, blow, it's Joanna! Timmy! Quick, hide!' whispered George, stuffing Timothy rapidly under the bedcovers. If the housekeeper saw him she would be bound to tell Father!

But it wasn't Joanna. When George opened the door Jack was standing there, shivering and looking very scared indeed.

'I w-w-wondered if I could come and sit in your room for a while,' stuttered the boy.

'What on earth for?' exclaimed George, scowling.

'I-I'm scared we'll be struck by lightning,' confessed Jack.

'Oh, for goodness' sake!' said George impatiently. 'Of course we won't.'

'We're the only house for miles around,' said Jack, still shivering. 'And lightning is attracted to high places, so we could be.'

'Well, sitting in my bedroom won't stop it, then, will it?' hissed George.

'N-n-no,' admitted Jack. 'Sh-shall I go back to my own room, then?'

George suddenly felt sorry him. She felt a little guilty too. She had told Mother she would try to be nice to him but she hadn't really made any effort at all.

'Oh, come in, then, if you must,' she said impatiently.

'Th-thank you,' said Jack. 'I didn't like to wake Joanna. She'd think I was an awful baby.'

'Well, you are,' said George. 'There's really nothing to be scared of. Look, come over to the window and watch the lightning, it's thrilling!'

'No, thanks,' said Jack, sounding just a little braver now. 'I'll just sit here on the bed.'

He sat down heavily on the side of George's bed. Suddenly there was a loud yowl and Jack jumped up again as if he had just sat on a pin.

'Oh, my goodness!' cried the startled boy as Timothy scrambled out from under the covers, his tail wagging nineteen to the dozen. He ran round the room jumping up first at George, then at Jack. 'Timmy!' he exclaimed. 'Are you scared of storms too? Is that why you're hiding?'

'No, of course he isn't,' said George impatiently. 'He's the bravest dog that ever lived. And if you tell anyone you've seen him here I'll tell your father about that boy in the village shop!'

'Of course I won't tell anyone,' said Jack, making a fuss of the puppy. 'Isn't he supposed to be here then?'

'No,' confessed George, telling Jack where Timothy was really supposed to sleep.

'What fun!' said Jack, grinning. 'I wish I had a dog to sleep on *my* bed.'

'Why *aren't* you allowed to have one?' asked George curiously. She forgot all about the storm for a minute and turned from the window. She sat down beside Jack and Timothy.

'We haven't got a garden or anything,' explained Jack. 'It wouldn't be fair to have a dog if there's no garden for him to play in.'

'No garden!' exclaimed George. 'How perfectly horrid.'

'It's quite nice where I live, actually,' said Jack. 'But we're not allowed to have pets.' He stroked Timothy and tickled him behind the ear. 'Still, I can pretend Timmy is mine while I'm here, can't I?'

'No, you jolly well can't,' said George indignantly. 'I'm sorry, but no-one can *pretend* to have Timmy. He's mine.'

Jack jumped as a bolt of lightning flashed very close by. Soon after, an enormously loud clap of thunder shook the whole house.

George ran to the window. 'For goodness' sake come and look, Jack! You can't be a baby all your life.'

'Oh, all right,' said Jack, suddenly feeling rather bold. He got up from the bed and went cautiously to the window. 'I suppose if you and Timmy aren't scared of thunder and lightning there's no reason why I should be either.'

'That's right,' said George. 'You're just being silly. This house is very old, you know. There have probably been millions of storms since it was built so there's really nothing to worry about.'

Just as Jack reached the window there was a dazzling flash of lightning and the whole beach was lit up.

George gasped. There was someone down there! Two figures, one smaller than the other, were hurrying along the sand carrying heavy spades and sacks across their shoulders.

'Did you see that, Jack?' she cried, turning to him in horror.

Jack *had* seen them. 'They were going towards Needle Rock,' said the boy, sounding shocked. 'And one of them looked like that boy I was talking to in the shop!'

Then George suddenly realized something. The two figures were the same people she had seen that afternoon, picking things up off the beach and throwing them into the water. It must have been the boy and his father looking for signs of the dinosaur bones!

'I bet they're going to dig for the bones,' she cried in horror.

'What would someone like that want old bones for?' asked Jack dubiously.

'To sell for money, of course, stupid!' said George.

'But he told me his father was rich and important,' said Jack.

'He was probably lying,' said George, frowning. 'What on earth are we going to do?'

'Supposing they do find the rest of them,' wailed Jack, looking very worried indeed. 'My dad will be absolutely furious. He'll never trust me again!'

'Well, there's only one thing we *can* do,' said George, suddenly feeling quite sorry for Jack. It really was jolly bad luck to have let the secret slip to just the wrong sort of person. 'We'll have to go down there and see what they're up to!'

'We-we can't possibly go *outside*,' stuttered Jack, looking scared again. 'We could get struck by lightning!'

'Well, we'll have to if we're going to save those bones, *and* save you from getting into lots of trouble,' said George determinedly.

Jack shook his head. 'I c-can't,' he stammered. 'I'm too frightened.'

'Oh, for goodness' sake go back to bed, then!' said George. 'Timmy and I will just have to go on our own, that's all!'

Jack climbed off her bed and slipped out of the door looking rather shamefaced. He padded along the corridor to his room and closed the door quietly. There was nothing else for it. George and Timothy would have to go out in the storm on their own.

11

Adventures in the night

'Wretched boy,' muttered George, still fuming about Jack as she flung on her trousers and a thick jumper over her pyjamas. She waggled her finger at Timothy. 'Now *don't* make a noise, Timmy. If you wake Joanna I'll be very angry!'

Timothy gave a very quiet little 'wuff' just to show he had heard what she said. This was very exciting! A walk in the dark! He was not at all sure what his little mistress was up to but he had a feeling that it was going to be something absolutely thrilling.

George put her finger to her lips as she crept along the landing past Joanna's bedroom.

She stopped for a moment and listened outside the door. She could hear Joanna's gentle snores and heaved a big sigh of relief. If the thunder hadn't woken her up then it wasn't likely she would hear them creeping down the stairs.

There was no sound from Jack's room either.

'I bet he's hiding under the covers,' she whispered to Timothy as they crept by. 'What a coward!'

Downstairs, George got her mackintosh from the hallstand and slipped her feet into her Wellington boots.

'Stay close to me, Timmy,' she hissed as they crept through the kitchen and out of the back door.

Outside, the wind was so strong it almost took away George's breath as she closed the back door softly and set off down the path.

Through the gate they went, on to the track that led down to the beach. George had been along the path hundreds of times and could find her way easily even on the darkest of nights.

The rain stung her face like needles and it wasn't long before Timothy's coat was very wet indeed. Overhead, the lightning flashed and the thunder roared. The storm didn't seem to be abating one bit.

The puppy kept very close to George's feet as she sped along the track and down towards the shore. The rain had made it rather slippery and once or twice she almost lost her balance.

They battled their way on to the beach where the waves were crashing on the shore in a torrent of white foam. Black thunder clouds scudded madly across the sky. George's eyes strained through the darkness to see the two figures. She had her little torch in her pocket but did not dare to put it on in case they were seen.

She spotted the two figures as the sky was lit by lightning once more. They were digging behind Needle Rock. It was certain now. They were trying to find the dinosaur bones!

The two adventurers crept towards them, keeping as close to the cliff base as they could. The wind whipped at George's dark curls and tore at her mackintosh. Her eyes and nose were full of salty spray and Timothy looked just like a drowned rat. He had to keep shaking his head as the water dripped into his eyes and he couldn't see where he was going.

The little dog was not at all sure he liked being out in the dead of night in such a terrible storm after all, even though he knew he had to protect his little mistress from any danger that might come their way.

'This way!' whispered George, and Timothy followed her into the shelter of a large rock some way from where the robbers were still digging as hard as they could. 'We can spy on them from here!'

George crouched down with Timmy beside her, her heart thudding like mad. She put her hand on the little dog's head so he would know he wasn't allowed to growl and bark. The storm was very noisy but if the intruders *did* hear him the two of them would be in *real* trouble.

'It *is* that boy from the village shop, Timmy!' hissed George.

'And an older man. I bet it's his father. They look like real villains to me!'

She was desperately racking her brains for ideas. She had to find a way to stop them finding the bones without giving herself and Timothy away.

As they watched, the storm at last began to abate. The thunder rolled away out to sea and the lightning flashes grew further and further apart. The two figures threw back the hoods of their mackintoshes and begin to dig even harder. Suddenly the youth bent down and picked something up. There was a flash of torchlight that revealed a large bone just like the one Timothy had dug up.

The boy's voice came towards them. 'This looks like one, Dad. There you are, what did I tell you!'

'Oh, blow!' exclaimed George in a whisper. 'They've found one. We've got to stop them, Timmy. We've just got to!'

Just then, Timothy gave a low, warning growl and, to her horror, she heard footsteps crunching on the sand behind her. Suddenly someone grabbed her from behind, putting their hand over her mouth. She tried to scream and yell but the hand was clamped so tightly she couldn't make a sound.

Her heart leapt with fear. Did the two robbers have an accomplice who had discovered her spying on them?

Then a voice hissed in her ear.

'It's all right, George, it's only me, don't make a noise.'

Her arms were released and she spun round. Jack was standing behind her looking very wet and bedraggled and rather sheepish.

'I couldn't let you come on your own after all,' he explained, shivering. 'I decided I'd risk getting struck by lightning and I didn't want you to call out in surprise when I turned up.'

He bent down and gave Timothy a quick stroke. The puppy licked his hand as if to say 'I'm really glad you're here!'

George scowled, angry she had allowed herself to be frightened. 'You scared me!' she whispered furiously.

'Sorry,' said Jack.

'Never mind,' said George, suddenly realizing exactly how brave Jack had been to put aside his fear of the storm and come out to help her. 'They've found a bone, I'm afraid. I saw it by the light of their torch.'

'Oh, blow!' said Jack. 'What are we going to do?'

'We've got to stop them but I've no idea how,' whispered George, shaking her head.

They crouched down behind the rock, watching the two villains at work. They were digging a very deep hole in the sand. Every now and then one of them pulled something out and they both examined it by torchlight, then put it into one of their sacks.

If George and Jack didn't hurry up and think of something quickly, the whole skeleton might soon be uncovered!

Suddenly Jack pulled George's arm and made her stand up. 'I've got an idea,' he whispered. 'Come on, let's go back!'

'We can't . . .' began George. 'We've . . .'

But the boy was already hurrying back along the base of the cliff towards the path.

To George's annoyance Timothy ran after him. Afraid he would bark to get her to follow, George ran to catch them up.

Soon, the three were safely back on the cliff path and hurrying towards Kirrin Cottage.

'What on earth are you doing!' cried George angrily. 'We can't just leave those horrid men to steal all the bones.'

'We're not going to,' said Jack. 'We're going to scare them away.'

'How?' asked George scornfully. 'They're a lot bigger than us!'

'Wait and see,' said Jack mysteriously.

To George's surprise, he led them towards the garden shed and threw open the door.

'You haven't got a torch, I suppose, have you?' he asked when they were inside.

'Of course I have,' said George, pulling her little torch from her pocket. 'I always carry it *and* my penknife and string. You never know when you're going to have an adventure and need things like that.'

'Good,' said Jack, sounding full of admiration. 'Shine it over here.'

George was astonished to see a most peculiar contraption in the corner of the shed. There were empty baked bean tins fished out of the dustbin and washed, pink painted cardboard cones and strips of silver paper and all manner of other things tied on to a long piece of strong string.

'What on earth is *that?*' exclaimed George.

'It's my bird scarer, silly,' said Jack. 'And if my plan works, it will be a thief scarer too!'

12

A terrific plan

George stared at the gadget with her hands on her hips. 'How on earth are we going to scare them with that thing?' she exclaimed scornfully.

Jack quickly explained how the bird scarer worked. A broad grin spread across George's face. If Jack was right, his device would scare away a whole horde of robbers, not just two!

'We could do with a whistle, too,' said Jack, looking thoughtful. 'I don't suppose you've got one, have you?'

'Of course,' said George, taking hers from her pocket. 'I always carry one of those too.'

Jack looked at George in amazement. He was obviously thinking what a remarkable little girl she was.

'Well done,' he said admiringly. 'Right, let's get back down to the beach.'

So the two brave children and the little shaggy dog picked up the extremely strange contraption and set off down the garden path once more.

Timmy ran on ahead, his shaggy tail waving like a banner. Now the storm had rolled away, it was very dark indeed but dogs could see very well in the dark and he was quite happy to lead the way!

George was so used to the path she didn't even hesitate but once or twice Jack stumbled and almost fell over on the slippery, stony track.

They had to be very careful not to let the tin cans rattle together and warn the robbers they were coming.

'Timmy, darling, heel!' hissed George as they hurried down the slope that led to the beach.

Timothy slowed his pace. He was dying to get on with the adventure. He had spotted the robbers too and was absolutely longing to bark and bark until they ran away.

They kept close to the base of the cliff as they crept towards Needle Rock.

The men were still digging furiously. They had balanced their torch on a smaller rock and were working in the beam of light. One of their sacks looked almost full up.

Suddenly their voices echoed towards the crouching children.

'Look at this one, Jim,' grunted the older man. 'It's a real whopper. Should be worth a fortune I reckon.'

The youth hurried over and together they tried to heave an enormous bone from the trench.

'We'll never get it out,' panted the man. 'We'll 'ave to come back for it another time.'

'Don't be daft, Dad,' replied the youth. 'Once they find out we've been 'ere they'll guard the site. It's now or never!' He began hacking away at the sand with his spade.

'Rotten devil!' hissed Jack angrily. 'He'll ruin it. You have to be very careful with these ancient bones.'

'We'd better get started then,' whispered George.

'Right,' agreed Jack.

'I'll creep round the back of the rock,' said George. 'I'll take one end of the scarer with me. You stay here. We'd both better start together.'

'Right,' said Jack. 'I'll start counting to a hundred when you set off. You do the same and when we get to a hundred we'll begin.'

'Good idea,' whispered George. 'Come on, Timmy, you come with me!'

George held the contraption very close to her chest as she and Timmy crept along in the shadow of the cliff, then across to Needle Rock. She hardly dared to breathe and her heart beat so hard it hurt. She managed to get very close to the men and could hear the crunch of their spades as they dug into the ground.

Timothy was as good as gold. He knew by the tone of his mistress's voice that it was very important to be quiet. He did not know how long he was going to be able to resist barking at the horrible strangers. He just hoped he could hold off until George told him it would be all right.

'Sixty-one . . . sixty-two . . . sixty-three . . .' murmured George to herself as she crouched behind Needle Rock. She breathed a huge, silent sigh of relief. The men had not spotted her or heard a single thing.

'Ninety-one . . . ninety-two . . . ninety-three . . .' George's heart was still beating like a drum. Would their plan work? If it didn't and the men discovered them, then things could get very nasty indeed!

'Ninety-nine . . . one HUNDRED!'

On the count of a hundred an awful din broke loose over the peaceful Kirrin Bay.

First of all a loud voice boomed across the sand. 'All right, you two, the game's up! You're surrounded, so it's no good trying to get away!'

Then a whistle blew loudly and a very fierce dog began barking madly. Another voice rang out from behind Needle Rock. 'You'd better hand those bones over to us now, you men. You're under arrest!'

There was a rattling and banging sound and a quite deafening whistle screeched out, sounding just like a police whistle.

The villains looked round in horror and fear, dropping their spades in shock.

'It's the police!' exclaimed Jim. 'Come on, Dad, run for it!'

'They've dogs and all!' yelled Jim's father as they both took to their heels and ran.

'After them, men!' came a loud, deep voice as the two villains sped off along the water's edge, running as fast as they possibly could. The fierce barking followed them and then a loud voice called.

'Quick, men! Don't let them get away!'

The two robbers left the sacks, turned and rushed across the sand and up to the base of the cliff. They both began to climb the rocky path, scrambling and slipping dangerously as they went.

The moon came out from behind a cloud just as the men disappeared over the top. Then a car's engine started up and with a roar the robbers skidded away across the moor towards the road.

Down below, George, Timmy and Jack were staring upwards.

'Hurrah!' shouted George, jumping up and down. 'We've saved the bones. Yippee!'

Jack was jumping up and down too and laughing his head off. 'They really thought the police were here and they were going to be arrested. What brilliant fun!'

'And they thought Timmy was a fierce police dog!' laughed George, bending down and giving Timothy a huge hug and a pat. 'Well done, Timmy. You were marvellous!'

'My scarer was pretty remarkable, don't you think?' asked Jack.

'Terrific!' said George. 'You're jolly clever, you know, Jack.' She picked up one of the cardboard cones and shouted through it. 'All right, you two, the game's up!' Her voice came out, deep and booming, magnified a hundred times by the shape of the cone. She collapsed with laughter again and Jack danced round with Timothy, who barked joyfully that their plan had worked so well.

'It was too dark to see their faces but I bet they were scared stiff,' said Jack, laughing too.

'Come on,' said George, gathering up the bird scarer. 'We'd better get back before Joanna wakes up and wonders where we've gone.'

'What about the bones?' asked Jack, looking worried. 'We don't want to leave them here, they might come back for them!' He tried to lift one of the sacks but it was so heavy he couldn't even get it off the ground.

'I know,' said George suddenly. 'There's a cave just along the end of the beach. Let's drag them along there and hide them until your father gets home and we can all come and collect them.'

'Jolly good idea,' said Jack.

So, together, George and Jack heaved and dragged the full sack of bones along to the end of the beach and hid it in the cave. Timothy tried to help but only succeeded in tearing a hole in the sack as he grabbed it in his mouth.

'It's all right, thanks, Timmy,' panted Jack. 'I think we can manage without you this time.'

George glanced at him and chuckled. Being with Jack was turning out to be jolly good fun after all!

13

The end of the adventure

It was getting light by the time the two sacks were safely hidden from sight.

George, Timothy and Jack walked back to Kirrin Cottage, laughing and chattering about their adventure. The storm had disappeared and it was going to be a lovely, bright day.

'Your dad will be pleased that the bones are safe,' said George as they went through the garden gate and down the path to the house.

'Yes,' said Jack, pulling a face. 'But he won't be very pleased when he finds out they only knew the bones were there because *I* gave away the secret.'

They piled the bird scarer back in the shed and went indoors.

Joanna was already up, putting the kettle on for her morning cup of tea. She was very surprised indeed to see them coming through the door. 'My, you three are up early,' she said. 'I wondered where Timmy was. I didn't realize you'd taken him for a walk.'

George glanced at Jack. Should they tell Joanna about their adventure?

But before she could decide whether to or not, Jack blurted it out. 'Some men were trying to steal the bones,' he said without thinking. 'We scared them away.'

'Scared them away?' said Joanna, looking shocked. 'How on earth did you do that?'

So they sat down in the kitchen, sipping mugs of Joanna's hot chocolate and told her all about it.

'A bird scarer?' she exclaimed. 'How did you frighten those villains with a *bird scarer?*'

'I made cones out of cardboard,' explained Jack. 'And when the wind blows through them they make a strange noise.'

'So we *shouted* through them,' said George, laughing. 'And our voices sounded terrifically loud. They thought lots of police had come to arrest them.'

'There are tins that rattle together and silver paper that flashes in the sunlight,' said Jack. 'It looks as if those things frighten robbers as well as birds.'

'And they thought Timmy was a police dog,' said George. 'Oh, Joanna, it was so funny to see them running away from a little puppy!'

'Well, you're all very brave,' said Joanna, wiping her eyes and laughing so much her chin wobbled. 'Your parents are going to be very proud of you, you know.'

'And we're proud of Timmy,' laughed George, giving her darling puppy a big hug. 'He loves adventures just as much as we do.'

'Well, if you're going to have any more,' said Joanna, trying to be stern, 'I hope they won't be in the middle of the night!'

It was lunch-time when George's parents and the professor arrived home. George had been brushing the sand out of Timothy's coat until it shone like gold. Jack had disappeared into the potting shed. There was a lot of hammering and banging coming from inside.

'Has everything been all right?' asked George's mother as she came through the door and put her suitcase down in the hall.

'Oh, yes, fine,' said George, giving her a hug. 'Actually we've had a bit of an adventure.'

'An adventure?' said her father, coming in behind her. 'What *kind* of an adventure?'

'I'll get Jack and we'll tell you all about it,' said George, rushing off to find her friend.

She went into the shed but Jack was nowhere to be seen. Then George spotted him standing beneath the tree-house.

'Everyone's home, Jack,' she called. 'And they want to hear about our adventure.' She stopped in her tracks. There was a rope hanging from the tree with a kind of sling attached to it. What on earth had Jack been inventing now? 'What's that?' she asked, looking very puzzled.

'It's a hoist for Timmy,' explained Jack. 'Look, you put him in this canvas sling I've made out of an old sack, then you go up the ladder and pull it up.'

'He'll bump into the trunk,' said George doubtfully.

'No, look, I've put a wheel at the top to act as a pulley,' said Jack, who had overcome his fear of heights and climbed the ladder to put it up there. 'He'll be up in a flash and won't come to any harm at all.'

They tried it out and it worked extremely well.

'Oh, Jack, it's wonderful,' exclaimed George, her eyes shining with joy. 'We can have heaps of fun now. Thanks very much!'

'That's all right,' mumbled Jack, going a bit red in the face.

'And you climbed the ladder too,' said George, suddenly remembering how frightened Jack had been of climbing up high.

Jack shrugged. 'Well, I thought if I could go out in a thundering great storm then I could easily climb up into a silly old apple tree.'

George laughed. 'Well done, Jack. You're braver than any boy I've ever known!'

'Wurf, wurf,' said Timothy, agreeing with his mistress. He loved it up in the tree-house. He could see further than any other dog in the world. What jolly good fun!

'Are you coming indoors to tell us about your adventure?' called George's mother from below. 'We're dying to hear what has happened.'

So, George, Timothy and Jack piled indoors to tell the story of their adventure all over again.

'My word, you two,' said George's father admiringly. 'You were very brave indeed.'

'You mean us *three*,' said George indignantly. 'We couldn't have done it without Timmy!'

'The sacks were too heavy for us to carry so we've hidden them in a cave,' said Jack. 'We'll all go down later to collect them, shall we?'

'We certainly will,' said his father. 'My team are arriving tomorrow. They'll be pleased to hear that some of the job has already been done for them!'

'Well, thank goodness none of you came to any harm and those villains didn't get away with any of the bones,' said George's father.

'Yes,' said Professor Ward. 'I feel sure the whole skeleton is there and it would have been awful if some of it went missing.'

'But how did they know the bones were there in the first place?' asked George's mother, looking puzzled. 'I thought it was supposed to be a secret.'

'Village gossip, I expect,' said George, hurriedly getting up out of her chair. 'Come on, Jack, let's play in the tree-house.'

'Righty-ho,' said Jack, giving her a grateful glance for not giving him away.

Down the garden they went again. Two children and a little, shaggy, bouncing dog.

George grinned as her friend Jack climbed the ladder and pulled Timothy up on to the platform. Jack was terribly clever. It didn't matter one little bit that he didn't like swimming, or fishing or sailing or things that boys usually like. It was quite enough for him to be awfully brainy!

George climbed the ladder and sat on the platform with her arm round Timothy.

'I hope we're going to have lots more adventures like that, Timmy, darling,' she whispered in his cocked ear, her vivid blue eyes shining with excitement.

'Will you write to me and tell me about them if you do?' asked Jack rather enviously.

'I'll try,' said George although she wasn't very good at writing letters.

'Thanks,' said Jack. 'That will be fun.'

'Not as much fun as actually having them,' said George, giving Timothy another hug. 'Will it, Timmy, darling?'

'Wuff,' said Timothy, agreeing as usual. Nothing in the world was as much fun as having adventures with George!

ADVENTURE
FACTS
GUIDE

DOG TRAINING

ADVENTURE FACTS GUIDE

Training should begin as soon as your puppy arrives home. It's much easier to start right away than try to undo bad habits later on. Make sure everyone in the family sticks to the same rules, otherwise you will just confuse your new pet.

In the wild, dogs live in packs. Pack leaders eat first and sleep in the best spots, so if you feed your dog from the table while you're eating and let it sleep on your bed or lie on the sofa, you are giving the message that your dog is a top member of the pack. This could make life difficult when your cute puppy grows into a 'teenager' and starts trying to take control.

Training should be based on praise and rewards, not punishments. Start with very simple commands and wait until your pet has mastered these before moving on. It can be useful to keep puppies on a lead during training, so they can't get distracted and wander off. Body language means more to dogs than words, so accompany your command with a hand signal and make sure everyone uses the same word and sign. Single words are best, so say 'Sit', rather than 'Sit down', and 'Come' instead of 'Come here'.

It's best to get puppies used to sleeping in their own beds right from the start.

BASIC COMMANDS

It's good to start by teaching puppies their names. Call your pet's name and hold up a treat close to your face. When you have your puppy's full concentration, hand over the treat and make a fuss of your dog. Continue this training, using treats, toys and praise, until you get your pet's attention whenever you call.

Next, it's a good idea to teach your puppy to sit. This will make grooming and putting on a collar and lead much easier. Apart from this, a dog that sits on command won't jump up at visitors and can be made to sit and wait at the kerb until it's safe to cross the road.

A puppy that comes when called should get a treat immediately.

First get your puppy's attention. Hold a treat close to the dog's nose then move it up and backwards. As the head follows the treat, the legs should bend and your pet will sit down. As the puppy is carrying out the movement say the word 'Sit', then hand over the treat the second your dog's bottom touches the floor. Pushing your puppy's bottom down is not a good idea because your pet may expect you to do this every time.

Teaching your puppy to come when called is one of the most important training exercises. It could save your dog's life in a dangerous situation, and it will certainly save you a lot of running about, chasing after your pet!

One of the first things to teach your puppy is to sit on command.

You can either teach this with two people, where one leads the dog away and the other calls his or her name, or on your own by holding the dog on a long lead, then calling your pet. Use the simple command 'Come'. Gradually increase the distance, then try the exercise with the dog running free. Dogs should always be rewarded as soon as they come back, so that they associate coming back to you with something nice.

Never punish your puppy for having an accident.

It's important for your pet to mix with other dogs and puppies.

HOUSE TRAINING

Most puppies aren't reliably house trained until they're about six months old. Choose a spot that will be your puppy's toilet area, and take your pet there regularly after eating, drinking and playing. Puppies should be praised and rewarded for going in the right place. Indoors, you can reduce the amount of cleaning by covering the floor of your puppy space with newspaper. Your pet should get used to going to the toilet on the paper, then you can gradually reduce the paper-covered area.

FOSSILS

Fossils are the preserved remains of ancient life. They can range from the skeletons of massive dinosaurs to tiny traces of microscopic plants. Fossilization takes millions of years – the earliest known fossils are about 600 million years old.

Trilobites were sea creatures that ranged in size from 6 mm (1/4 inch) to over 0.60 cm (2 feet) long. They became extinct 248 million years ago.

This ammonite may have been swimming with mosasaurs and plesiosaurs 70 million years ago.

Most fossils are found in sedimentary rocks, such as limestone, sandstone or shale, which are made up of tiny particles that have settled at the bottom of an ocean, lake or river. Because sedimentary rock normally forms where water is present, the most common fossils are the remains of aquatic creatures like fish, trilobites and ammonites (squid-like molluscs with spiral shells).Typically, a fossil forms when a creature dies and its body is covered by layers of sediment. Over thousands of years, the sediment turns into rock and the creature is fossilized within it. In most cases, only the harder parts of a body, such as bones, teeth or shells, survive, but occasionally skin, fur or feathers can be found.

Amber is fossilized tree resin. This grasshopper became trapped in the sticky sap millions of years ago.

Other fossils are traces of living things, such as footprints, dung (coprolites), burrows or nests. Fossils also include insects trapped in amber and creatures preserved in tar or ice.

This footprint was made by a duck-billed dinosaur that lived in Colorado, USA, during the Cretaceous period.

FOSSIL HUNTING

It is easier to find fossils than you might think, as long as you look in the right place. You need to find an area where the sedimentary rock has been exposed, for example, a cliff face eroded by the sea, or an excavation site, like a quarry. But there are some important rules to follow before you start looking.

- **Never go fossil hunting alone – always take an adult with you.**
- **Don't climb in dangerous areas and avoid places where there are loose rocks.**
- **Stay away from cliff edges.**
- **If you are near the sea, beware of getting cut off by the tide.**
- **Wear sensible, protective clothing, sturdy boots, and a helmet if there's any risk of falling rocks.**
- **If the site is on private land, ask the owner's permission first.**
- **The best way to search for fossils is to join a club. It's more fun and you can learn a lot from the other members.**

DINOSAURS

ADVENTURE FACTS GUIDE

Dinosaurs lived on Earth for 180 million years – in comparison, humans have only been here for about five million. The age of dinosaurs, known as the Mesozoic era, began with a massive extinction, called the 'great dying', when 95 per cent of all living things were wiped out. The cause remains a mystery, but gradually, over millions of years, plant life returned, along with insects, amphibians, turtles, small mammals and the first dinosaurs.

Plateosaurus was a long-necked, plant-eating dinosaur from the late Triassic period.

The Triassic period, when dinosaurs first appeared, lasted from 245 to 213 million years ago. The Earth looked very different then. All the continents were joined together in one giant landmass, called Pangaea. One of the earliest dinosaurs was Eoraptor, a small meat-eater from what is now South America.

The Triassic period ended with another extinction. There were huge volcanic eruptions and the supercontinent of Pangaea began to break up. Many early dinosaurs died out, but others adapted and evolved.

The Jurassic period that followed lasted from 213 to 144 million years ago. Pangaea split into two mega-continents: Laurasia and Gondwana, and dinosaurs flourished. Herds of giant long-necked sauropods, like Brachiosaurus and Diplodocus, roamed the forests of conifers and tree ferns, while fierce meat-eater, Allosaurus, preyed on plant-eaters, such as Stegosaurus.

Stegosaurus was as big as a lorry, but its brain was the size of a walnut.

Allosaurus was a powerful predator with dozens of sharp, serrated teeth and could even ambush the giant sauropods, like Apatosaurus.

During the Cretaceous period, from 144 to 65 million years ago, the landmass broke up still further and the new continents drifted apart, so by the late Cretaceous, the world looked similar to the way it does today. Flowering plants appeared and the climate grew warmer. This was the golden age of dinosaurs. Many new species evolved, including the huge meat-eaters, Tyrannosaurus rex and Giganotosaurus, the horned ceratopsians, like Triceratops, and the fast-running pack hunters, such as Velociraptor and Deinonychus.

At the end of the Cretaceous period, all the dinosaurs suddenly became extinct. Most scientists believe that they perished after a meteor the size of Mount Everest hit the Earth. The impact would have caused massive fires and tidal waves, and thrown dust and debris into the atmosphere, blocking out the sunlight. Without the sun, the plants would all have died, followed by the plant-eating dinosaurs and, eventually, the meat-eaters that preyed on them.

Tyrannosaurus had 50 to 60 thick, conical, bone-crunching teeth and preyed on Triceratops and other plant-eating dinosaurs.

HOW TO CRACK CODES

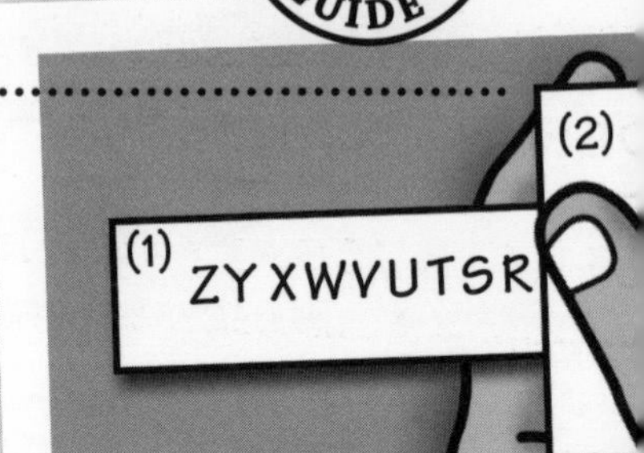

Remember that the person receiving your code will need the key you used to write your message, or they won't be able to decode it.

SLIDER CODE

You will need:

> **Two sheets of A4 paper with squares printed on them**
> **Scissors**
> **Pencil or pen**

The letters need to be evenly spaced so they line up properly. The easiest way to do this is to use paper with 5 mm squares printed on it and write the letters in the squares. You can download squared paper from the internet.

1. Write the alphabet backwards twice on one line, starting at Z, in the centre of the paper. You will need to turn the paper so the longest side is facing you, otherwise the letters won't all fit. This will be sheet 1.
2. On your second sheet of paper, write the alphabet once, in the right order, about one centimetre (2 squares) higher than the letters on your first sheet. This will be sheet 2.
3. Ask an adult to cut a rectangle shape out of the centre of sheet 2, just below the alphabet, as shown above.
4. Put sheet 2 on top of sheet 1, so you can see the letters on sheet 1 through the slot.

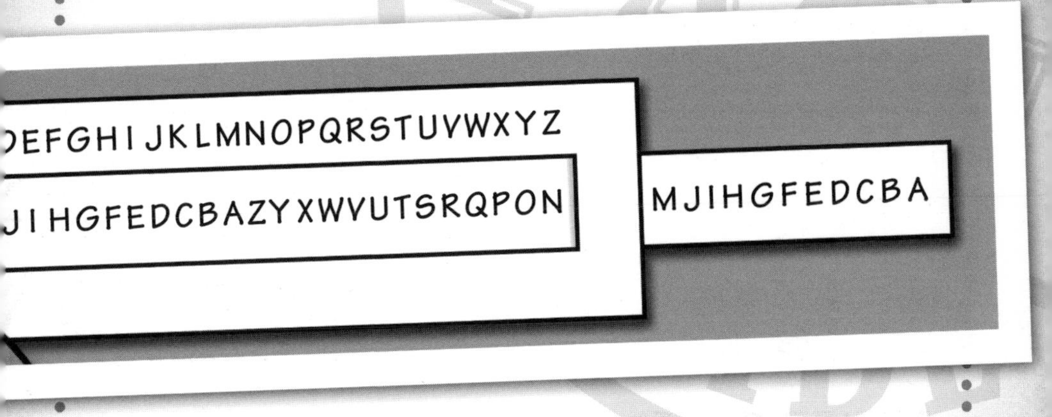

DEFGHIJKLMNOPQRSTUVWXYZ

JIHGFEDCBAZYXWVUTSRQPON

MJIHGFEDCBA

5. Choose a letter on sheet 1 that will be your code key (M, for example) and position the letter A on sheet 2 above your code key letter. This means that M will equal A, L will equal B, etc. You will need to let the receiver of the message know your code key letter.

To write your message in code, select the letters on sheet 2 and see which letter lines up with it in the slot below. Replace the letters of your message with those that appear within the slot on sheet 1.

CRACK IT

The person who receives the message will need to make their own slider decoder as shown above. Apart from that, they just need to know your chosen code key letter to crack the code.

GET CRACKING!

Use the slider decoder to decipher the message below using the code key letter H.

BDTQBD ZP LHZOZUB HO ATVD

Answers on page 333.

RULER CODE

You will need:

> **Paper**
> **Ruler**
> **Pencil or pen**

1. Lay a ruler across a sheet of paper and write the letters of your message at every centimetre mark.
2. Make a mark on the last letter of your message – either draw a circle around the letter or draw a line underneath it. This tells the reader where the message ends.
3. Fill in the spaces between the letters of your message with other letters (these can be any letters you like).

CRACK IT

To read the message, place a ruler under the letters, making sure that the last letter is over a centimetre mark on the ruler. Now read the letters that appear at every centimetre mark.

GET CRACKING!

Use the ruler code to decipher the message below.

T G H S E L G W O K L C D U I F S D L I O L S Q (T)

0 1 2 3 4 5 6 7 8 9 10 11 12

ROUTE CODE

You will need:

> **Two pieces of paper**
> **Pencil or pen**

Draw a grid that has five squares across and five squares down on each piece of paper.

On one piece of paper draw a line through the boxes with a red pen, as shown below, and give this to the person receiving the message. This is known as the route key.

Following the line you have drawn, write your message on the blank grid on the other piece of paper.

H	E	L	D	W
D	L	O	S	O
N	P	E	T	N
E	T	H	A	E
S	O	T	B	L

The more complicated the line you draw, the harder your message will be to decipher.

CRACK IT

Look at the route key and follow the path around the letters of the message.

GET CRACKING

Using the route key here try to crack the code in the box.

MASK

You will need:

- > **Tracing paper**
- > **Pencil**

A masked message can only be decoded by using a special overlay of card or paper (called a mask) with slots cut out of it. Without the mask, the message, if it is well written, will appear to be a completely innocent piece of text. For example, in the section below, a coded message is hidden.

If I can learn how to crack a code, anyone can – even you! All it takes is a love of language and the patience to follow a step-by-step method. The first thing to do is figure out what kind of code you are trying to solve. If you have a letter with a secret message hidden in it, then you have the type of code where you must find which words are part of the coded message, and which words are just there to hide the messages.

To crack this code you will need to trace the mask here and lay it over the message. The coded words in the message will be revealed through the holes in the mask.

Answers on page 333.

CODED CROSSWORD

Crack the number code to solve this crossword puzzle. As you work out which letter should replace each of the numbers, write them in the empty grid below. The answers are all names of animals and there's a clue below to get you started.

[1] 6	4	2	3		[2] 11	8	[3] 1
3							5
7		[4] 2		[5] 7	3	3	2
[6] 1	5	4	9				8
3		9		[7] 12			10
6			[8] 7	5	1		10
5				10			4
[9] 1	8	2	4	13	13	3	

1 DOWN > This animal is very prickly.

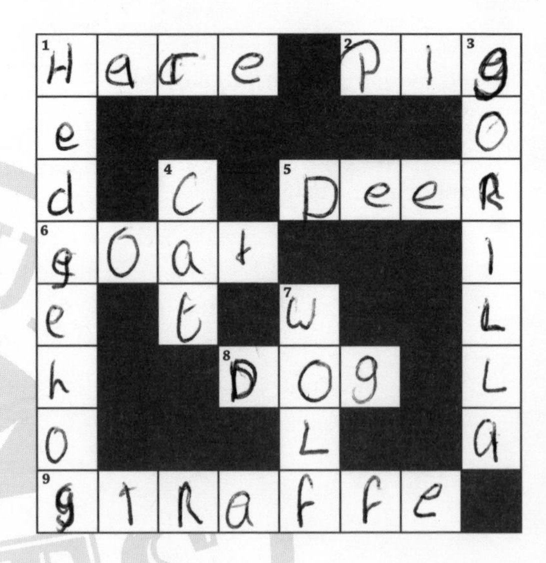

Answers on page 333.

The Footprint in the Sand

1

Trouble!

Timothy, the puppy, was in trouble again.

'It's no good, Georgina!' shouted George's father, waving a rather chewed and sorry-looking walking-stick. 'This is my best stick. That dog will have to go!'

George scowled. She detested being called by her full name and usually refused to answer. Georgina was a girl's name and she simply hated being a girl.

'He didn't *mean* to chew it, Father,' she cried. 'He thought it was one of his own sticks.'

Since George, a rather extraordinary little girl with very short, dark curls and vivid sky-blue eyes, had found the puppy and brought him home, he had often been in trouble. The main problem was that chewing was Timothy's favourite pastime and he simply could not resist it.

'Well, he'll have to stay outside, then,' said George's father, his dark brows meeting together in a fierce frown. 'I won't have him in the house if he can't be trusted.' He stared down at George. George's father was very tall and rather terrifying. He had dark hair and eyes and a very strong temper, exactly like George. The two often quarrelled, though they loved one another dearly.

'All right, then,' exclaimed George huffily. 'I'll go outside too and I'll never come back indoors ever again!'

With that, the little girl picked up her naughty puppy and stormed out into the garden, slamming the kitchen door behind her.

George ran down the garden feeling very angry. She climbed the ladder to her tree-house, then hoisted Timothy up in his special sling. They both sat inside the house, staring moodily out over the sea. It just wasn't fair. Puppies couldn't *help* chewing things, it was their nature.

George lived in a house called Kirrin Cottage, though it was really too big to be a cottage. Her father was a famous scientist and worked in his study at the end of the house. The house had wonderful old white stone walls, a wooden front door and a lovely garden full of roses and vegetables. It sat on top of a low cliff overlooking the curve of golden sand in Kirrin Bay. The family had owned the house for many years and neither George, nor her parents, could imagine living anywhere else.

Guarding the entrance to the bay was a little rocky island with a wonderful, mysterious ruined castle right slap-bang in the middle. It had been built in olden times, tall and steadfast, to guard the coast from invaders. George loved playing on the island and often rowed there through the dangerous rocks in her little wooden boat.

George was not like a typical little girl. Most of all in the world she wanted to be a boy. She had even cut off her hair so that she would look like one. She could climb trees, whistle, run, swim and sail as good as any boy you could ever meet. She had found Timothy, a shaggy brown puppy with big ears and melting, toffee-coloured eyes, alone on the moor and no-one had ever claimed him. Now, he was her very best friend and she could not think what it would be like to be without him.

George's father had allowed her to keep Timothy at Kirrin Cottage on condition the little dog behaved himself. The trouble was, he hardly ever did!

'Never mind, Timmy, darling,' George said as they sat in the tree-house. She gave him an enormous hug. 'Father will forget all about his stick and you'll soon be allowed back indoors again.'

George's father was very absent-minded and often forgot things, so she hoped this would be true.

'Wuff,' said Timothy sadly. He loved living at Kirrin Cottage but would hate to have to live outside and not be with his beloved little mistress every single minute of the day.

George and Timothy had been sitting in the tree-house for a while when they heard George's mother calling them.

'I'm here, Mummy!' shouted George, peering out from the window of her tree-house. Her mother stood beneath the old apple tree where the house was nailed to a broad branch.

'Oh, there you are, you two,' she said, smiling at the two rather cheeky faces peering down at her. 'What was Father shouting about?'

George put Timothy in his sling and lowered him carefully to the ground. Then she clambered down the ladder and stood in front of her mother with her hands on her hips. 'Timmy chewed his walking-stick, that's all,' explained the little girl indignantly. 'But he didn't mean to. He thought it was one of his *own* sticks.'

'Wuff, wuff,' added Timothy, wagging his plumy tail at George's mother. She was his favourite person next to George. She never shouted at him like the tall, rather forbidding man whose name was Father.

'Oh, dear,' said George's mother with a sigh. 'You really will have to keep an eye on him, you know, George.'

'I *do* keep an eye on him,' protested her daughter indignantly.

'Well, then you'll have to keep *two* eyes on him,' said the kind woman, smiling. She was quite used to battles between George and her husband and had learned not to take them too seriously. 'You know you're only allowed to keep him here if he behaves himself.'

'He does *try*,' insisted George, bending to give Timothy another hug. 'Don't you, Tim?'

'Wurf,' said Timothy, looking up at Mummy from under his shaggy eyebrows.

George's mother couldn't help smiling again at her fiery daughter and the little puppy. 'Now,' she said, glancing at her watch. 'We're having visitors this afternoon so I want you to get changed please, George, and be on your best behaviour.'

'Get changed!' exclaimed George, looking down at her rather grubby shorts and plimsolls. 'What on earth for?'

'Because you look very untidy,' insisted her mother. 'A woman named Mrs Barratt has just moved into the village and I've asked her to tea. If she sees you like this she'll think I've got a messy little boy instead of a girl.'

'Well, that's just what I want people to think,' said George, scowling fiercely.

'Yes, I know,' said her mother patiently. 'But I've told her I've got a daughter so I want you to look like one. Put on that blue dress I bought when I visited your aunt and uncle.' George had an uncle and aunt and three cousins who lived in London. The cousins were called Julian, Dick and Anne but she had never met them and did not particularly want to. Especially as one of them was a girl! Girls were usually weak and babyish and she had no wish to meet *anyone* like that!

'I'm not wearing that dress!' said George disgustedly. 'It's perfectly horrid.'

Her mother gave another big sigh. Sometimes the battles with her daughter made her quite tired. 'Well, at least put some clean clothes on,' she said. 'They're coming at three o'clock.'

'Who's *they?*' enquired George. 'I thought you said it was a lady, Mrs Something-or-other?'

'Mrs Barratt,' said Mummy. 'And her little girl, Holly.'

'Holly!' exclaimed George, horrified. 'A *girl*!'

'Yes,' said her mother going back indoors. 'A *girl* – and I want you to be nice to her, please, George. Just for once, can't you do as you're told?'

'Sorry, Mummy, but I've promised to take Timmy for a walk,' said George as the idea popped into her head. 'So I might be out all afternoon!'

With that, the naughty girl ran off through the garden calling to her puppy. 'Come on, Timmy, I'll race you to the beach!'

Her poor mother gave another sigh, raised her eyebrows and went back indoors.

2

Visitors

Down the beach path George and Timothy went, running and skipping in the summer sunshine. With the bright blue sky above, and the birds singing, it really was heavenly. Suddenly, a rabbit ran across the path in front of them. Timothy immediately darted after it, barking his head off.

'Come back, Timmy!' called George. 'You don't want to get lost again.'

Timothy soon gave up his chase and scampered back to his small mistress. He loved being out on the moor but had never forgotten the time when he had been lost and George had rescued him. Now, he never strayed far from her side.

They jumped down the last bit of the path and ran along the sand. It was a lovely calm day and tiny waves swished and whooshed as they broke on the shore in little sprays of white foam. How lovely to be out in the fresh air on such a beautiful, warm day, thought George, taking a big breath of fresh sea air.

The two skipped down to the water's edge, then ran along to the tall, jagged rocks where the cliff came right down to the shore. They played hide-and-seek for a while, then went to explore the rockpools. They both adored gazing into them and trying to touch the tiny shrimps and scarlet sea-anemones that waved with the movement of the water.

'I'm not being nice to any *girl*,' said George sulkily to Timothy as they sat on a rock watching a flock of seagulls skim the surface of the waves. 'What on earth does Mummy want to invite a girl to tea for?'

'Wuff,' said Timothy, gazing up at her. He could tell his mistress was upset and pressed himself close to her to try to cheer her up. He hated it when George was unhappy.

George sat with her arm round him. 'Mummy's always trying to find me human friends,' she said. 'But I don't need anyone else when I've got you, do I, Tim?'

'Wuff,' agreed Timothy. He always knew every word that George was saying.

After a while George decided she really had better go back to Kirrin Cottage. She was already in her father's bad books because of the walking-stick episode. It probably wasn't a good idea to get into her mother's bad books too!

'Come on, Timmy,' she said, getting reluctantly to her feet. George often lost her temper and went off in a huff but usually got over it very quickly. Now she'd cooled down she knew she must go home and face the visitors.

Timothy barked and ran on ahead. He was quite looking forward to someone coming to tea. If he sat by their feet and gazed up at them, perhaps they would give him a piece of their sandwich!

When they got back to Kirrin Cottage the visitors had already arrived. Joanna, the woman who helped Mummy in the house, was in the kitchen preparing tea. There were cucumber sandwiches, rosy fresh tomatoes from the garden, crisp celery, a plate of custard cream biscuits, a huge fruit cake and a chocolate sponge.

George's mouth watered as she saw the delicious spread laid out ready to be taken into the garden. It had been ages since lunch-time and she was famished.

Joanna slapped her hand as she tried to pinch a biscuit on her way through. 'Your mother has left instructions that you're not to have any tea until you've changed,' she said.

Joanna was a round, jolly-faced person who was usually smiling all the time. Today, though, she looked rather stern.

'Oh please, can I just have one, Joanna?' asked George. 'Then I'll go and get changed, I promise.'

'Oh very well, then, dear,' said the woman, giving in, a smile twitching at the corners of her mouth. 'Just *one*, but don't tell anybody!'

'We won't, will we, Timmy?' said the little girl, grinning. She took a custard cream and ran upstairs with Timothy at her heels. If he was very good perhaps he might get a bit of biscuit before he even met the visitors!

'Now don't make a sound, Timmy,' whispered George. 'If Father hears you he might remember he's banned you from the house!'

Luckily, though, her father's study was right at the other end of the house. He didn't hear George and her puppy running up the stairs and into her little bedroom with its sloping roof and side window overlooking the sea.

George ignored the horrid blue dress that her mother had laid out on the bed. Instead she pulled on a clean pair of jeans and a shirt, then tried to comb the tangles out of her hair with her fingers. She licked her thumb and wiped a smudge of dirt off her nose.

'That'll do,' she said to Timothy. 'Come on, let's get it over with.'

The two ran down the stairs and through the sitting-room out into the garden where Joanna was laying the tea.

'Oh, George, *there* you are!' exclaimed her mother as George stood in the doorway, leaning against the frame with a scowl on her face.

A tall, thin lady wearing very fashionable clothes, a straw hat and scarlet lipstick, was sitting in a deckchair. She looked at George in surprise.

Next to her was another deckchair with its back to George. She could just see two legs poking out from underneath. Two legs ending in feet wearing pale blue sandals and snowy white ankle socks. Then a small face framed with long, straight hair peered round the edge of the chair.

It was the woman's daughter and she was wearing a pale yellow dress with frills at the sleeves and the neck. George thought it was the most revolting outfit she had ever seen.

'George!' said her mother. 'Come and meet Mrs Barratt and Holly.'

'Well, well, Fanny,' said the woman to George's mother. 'I was sure you said you had a little girl.'

'Her name's really Georgina,' explained Mummy with a smile. 'It's just that . . .'

But there was no further chance to explain because just then Timothy came hurtling through the door. He had lingered near the kitchen hoping for a titbit from Joanna and now ran to catch up with George.

As he dashed out into the garden, Holly gave a loud cry. 'A dog!' she screamed very loudly indeed. 'Mummy! Mummy! Save me!' She jumped out of the chair and ran over to her mother.

Oh, no! thought George. What a silly baby being scared of a puppy. This tea party is going to be *much* worse than I thought!

3

George in disgrace

'It's all right, dear,' said George's mother hastily as the little girl screamed. 'He's only a puppy. He won't hurt you.'

Timothy was looking amazed. No-one had ever *shrieked* when they saw him before.

'Take him away,' insisted Holly, still looking very scared. Timothy was wagging his tail and grinning at her with his little pink tongue hanging out.

'I'm so sorry,' said Mrs Barratt. 'But Holly's terrified of dogs.'

'Take him out the back and tie him up, George,' said George's mother. 'We can't have him frightening our guests.'

'I'm not tying him up!' declared George indignantly. 'It's his garden, not hers! And he didn't frighten *anyone*. She's just being a silly baby.'

'I'm sorry, dear, but visitors come first,' said her mother firmly. 'So please do as I say, Georgina.'

Georgina! That was the last straw. Out stormed George with a sad-looking Timothy at her heels. He simply could not understand what he had done wrong.

'I'm sorry, Timmy, darling,' said George, fetching a rope from the potting shed. She tied it to the puppy's collar. 'I'll get you a sandwich and a biscuit and bring them to you as soon as I can.' She tied the other end of the rope round one of the apple trees. She hated leaving him but she knew there were times when you simply had to do as you were told even if you hated it.

In the front garden, Holly seemed to have recovered from her scare. She was sitting back in the deckchair with a plate full of sandwiches, cake and biscuits on her lap. She pulled a face at George as she came stomping back, scowling at everyone from beneath her dark brows. What a baby Holly was. Fancy being scared of a puppy!

'My husband is opening a new antique shop in the next-door town,' said Mrs Barratt to George's mother. 'We're going to be awfully busy for the next few weeks.'

'That's nice,' replied Mummy. 'Holly can always come here and play with George if you need someone to look after her while you're helping your husband.'

That made George scowl even more. She had been hoping this would be Holly's one and only visit to Kirrin Cottage. Now it looked as if she might be coming again! It really was too bad!

When tea was finished, Joanna came to clear away the things. George had managed to hide three biscuits and a piece of chocolate cake in her pockets for Timothy. She knew it was bad for him to have titbits but *something* had to make up for being tied to a tree all afternoon!

'Why don't you show Holly your swing and the tree-house,' said Mummy. 'I'm going to take Helen round the garden to see my lovely roses.'

George sniffed and screwed up her nose. Someone who was scared of dogs was bound not to like tree-houses!

'Go along, Holly, dear,' said Mrs Barratt. 'And mind you don't get your dress dirty.'

Holly had not spoken a word to George during tea. In fact she had been in an awfully bad sulk too. The two little girls sat face to face now, both scowling and frowning at one another.

'Where is this tree-house, then, *Georgina?*' asked Holly rudely as they went round to the back garden.

'I don't answer to that name,' said George haughtily.

'Why not?' asked Holly, flicking back her long hair over her shoulder.

'Because I don't, that's all. I only answer to George,' said George.

'Oh, all right then, *George*,' said Holly. 'Where is this famous tree-house of yours?'

'It's not famous at all,' said George. 'And it's in a tree. Where else would it be, silly? You have to climb a ladder to get into it.'

'I'm not going up there,' declared Holly when she saw the house and the old wooden ladder reaching up into the branch. 'Mummy will kill me if I get my dress dirty.'

'Please yourself,' said George, going over to Timothy, who had already smelled his titbits and was barking excitedly.

Holly gave the puppy a wide berth as George crouched down.

She pulled the rather squashed food from her pockets. Timothy soon gobbled it all up, then stuck his nose into George's pocket to lick up all the crumbs which had got left behind.

'I'm going to let him off,' said George when Timothy had finished clearing out her pocket. 'He's fed up with being tied up.'

Holly looked very scared as George untied the rope. Timothy ran eagerly towards her. Now was his chance to make friends with this new little girl.

'Oh,' shrieked Holly, rapidly scrambling up the tree-house ladder. The thought of Timothy jumping up at her was much more frightening than climbing so high. 'I won't come down until you tie him up again,' she called down from above.

'All right,' said George. 'Stay up there, then. We're going to have a game of ball.' And she went and got Timothy's ball from the shed and began playing with him.

First she made him sit still. 'Stay!' she commanded. She threw the ball as hard as she could across the lawn. Timothy quivered with excitement. This was one of his favourite games but he wasn't allowed to get the ball until his mistress said so.

He looked up at her with his melting brown eyes. 'Right, Timmy,' said George, grinning down at him. 'Now . . . *fetch*!'

The puppy shot off down the garden like a rocket. He picked up the ball and brought it back, laying it at George's feet.

'Good boy!' She gave him a big hug. 'Clever boy!' Then she threw the ball again.

A little while later her mother came round to the back garden with Mrs Barratt.

'Time to go, now,' the woman said. She stopped when she saw George playing with Timothy. Her daughter was nowhere in sight. Where on earth had the little girl gone?

'I'm up here, Mummy,' called Holly from the tree-house.

'Oh, Holly, whatever have you been up to? Look at your dress, it's filthy!' cried her mother, looking up and frowning.

George held on to Timothy's collar while Holly clambered down the ladder. She stood at the bottom looking sulky. Her dress had black and green streaks all down the front. 'Sorry, Mummy,' she said, hanging her head so her long hair covered her face.

George's mother guessed what had happened and felt very angry. 'Go to your room at once, George!' she said sternly. Her mother was always very fair and usually gave George a chance to explain but this time she was embarrassed and very annoyed indeed.

'But I didn't . . .' began George.

'NOW, Georgina!' insisted her mother. 'And tie Timothy up again before you leave, please!'

George put her puppy back on his rope. 'It wasn't my fault,' she muttered, even though she knew it was.

'I'm so sorry, Helen,' apologized her mother. 'I don't know what's got into George, letting Holly get dirty like that.'

Holly stood looking at her feet and did not say a word.

'Don't worry, Fanny,' said Mrs Barratt. 'I'll make sure Holly wears something more suitable tomorrow.'

'Tomorrow!' said George, scowling to herself as she stomped indoors and up the stairs in the biggest huff she had been in for ages. 'Surely she's not coming again tomorrow! How perfectly frightful!'

4

George and Timothy escape

When she got upstairs, George slammed her bedroom door as hard as she could so that everyone would know what a bad mood she was in.

She stomped over to her bed and plonked herself down, frowning and staring out over the moor. Actually, she felt rather guilty. She had been horrid to Holly and had got her into trouble. But it was just so awful when grown-ups made you do things you didn't want to do! Why couldn't they just leave her and Timothy alone? That was what she wanted most in the world. Being all on her own with her beloved puppy and no-one to interfere or tell them what to do.

She was still feeling miserable when her mother came into the room.

'I was very disappointed in you today, George,' she said, looking very sad indeed.

'Sorry, Mummy,' mumbled George. 'But that girl was so *babyish* to be scared of Timmy.'

'Well, she's coming again tomorrow,' said her mother firmly. 'So I'm afraid Timmy will have to be tied up again.'

George glowered at her mother and didn't answer. Tying Timothy up was more than she could bear. She simply wouldn't let that happen. She would have to find a way to escape for the day!

George was already making a plan in her head as she lay in bed that night. The house was silent. All she could hear was the sound of the waves on the shore. Her parents had gone to bed and Timothy was in his usual place by the stove in the kitchen. It would soon be safe to go and fetch him.

George's father didn't allow Timothy to sleep on George's bed so each night after everyone was asleep she slipped down the stairs and fetched him up to her room. Then, in the morning, she would get up early and put him back in the kitchen. Father never asked where Timothy slept so George never had to tell him. The little girl never told lies so she would have had to confess if her father *had* ever suspected.

When she knew it was safe, George threw back her covers and slipped out of her room. She tiptoed down the stairs. She couldn't wait to tell Timothy all about the plan she had made.

The puppy was waiting quietly by the door as George crept into the kitchen. This was one of his favourite games. Lying down by the stove until his mistress appeared, then creeping up the stairs and into her room when she came for him. Great fun!

'Now, Timmy,' whispered George, when the little dog was safely tucked up in her bed, 'this is what we're going to do tomorrow when that horrid girl comes again . . .'

'Wuff,' said Timothy very softly. He loved it when George whispered secrets into his ear. It always meant they were going to have an adventure.

'We'll get Joanna to pack us a picnic and we'll spend the day on Kirrin Island,' hissed George. 'That horrid girl will never find us there!'

Timothy's ears pricked up when he heard the words Kirrin Island. George had been promising to take him there for ages.

'We'll have great games, Timmy,' said George, cuddling him. 'I'll show you the castle and the two ruined towers!'

'Wuff,' said Timothy, his tail going thump, thump on the mattress. His little heart went pit-a-pat with excitement.

'And we'll explore inside,' George went on, stroking Timmy's soft head. 'There's an exciting room with an old stone fireplace. We can pretend we're soldiers guarding the entrance to the bay.' She gave the puppy a hug. 'Oh, Timmy, we're going to have such a thrilling time!'

There was a beautiful blue sky when George woke up in the morning. It was going to be another perfect summer day.

She sat up and stretched, gazing out of the little window that overlooked the sparkling sea. She felt a thrill of excitement. One of her favourite things in all the world was playing on Kirrin Island.

The island had belonged to her mother's family for many years and she had promised that one day it would belong to George.

Suddenly a large flock of seabirds rose up from the island shore with cries and squawks of alarm. Then came a very strange flash of light as if someone was shining a torch in broad daylight.

'Timmy, did you see that?' exclaimed George, looking very puzzled. What on earth could the strange light be?

Timothy jumped up with his paws on the windowsill. He couldn't see anything except the sky and the sunshine and a flock of gulls whirling and diving in the air.

'Something has scared those birds,' said George with a frown. 'I wonder what it was?'

She watched for a while but soon the gulls settled back down on the other side of the island and everything went quiet again.

George shrugged. 'Oh well, Timmy, it was probably nothing.'

It was still early and her parents were fast asleep. George quickly pulled on her jeans and shirt and slipped downstairs and out into the garden with Timothy. Joanna was coming down the garden path, pushing her bicycle.

'Joanna, could we have a picnic today, please? We're going to the island,' said George, running up to her.

Timothy barked and bounced along beside Joanna, growling and trying to bite the tyres of her bicycle.

'Well, it's a lovely day for it,' said Joanna, smiling at Timothy's fierce growls and barks. 'So I don't see any reason why not if your mother says it's all right.'

'Oh . . . don't bother Mummy,' said George hurriedly. 'I'll leave her a note to tell her where we've gone.'

'Very well,' said Joanna.

'We're going very soon,' said George. 'Would it be all right to do our picnic straightaway?'

'One thing at a time,' said Joanna, parking her bicycle by the back door. 'I'll get your breakfast first.'

After breakfast, George hurriedly scribbled a note and popped it under her parents' bedroom door.

'I'm having a picnic on the island,' wrote George. *'I don't think Holly would enjoy playing with me today but she can play with my things if she likes.'*

George was a very generous little girl at heart even though she didn't really think Holly would like playing with toy cars and trains. George thought she was more the type who played with dolls and teddy bears, the very things she hated!

Joanna packed up George's rucksack with lots of delicious things. There were tomato sandwiches, cake and biscuits, a bottle of homemade ginger beer, some water and biscuits for Timothy.

'Thanks, Joanna,' said George, shrugging on the rucksack. 'Come on, Timmy, let's go!'

George felt a small pang of guilt as she and Timmy set off along the path to the beach. Mummy was *not* going to be very pleased when she learned George would not be there to play with Holly.

'We can't help it though, can we, Timmy?' said the little girl, pulling a wry face. 'I'm simply not going to let you be tied up all day because of a silly girl!'

'Wuff,' barked Timothy, scampering on ahead. Hurrah! They were going to the island. He had the feeling this was going to be a very thrilling day indeed!

5

On their way!

In Kirrin Bay, George's little wooden boat was pulled high up on the sand. Timothy jumped in and sat in the bow. His tail wagged like a flag and his pink tongue lolled out. He sniffed the salty air and felt a thrill of excitement.

George put her rucksack on the seat and pushed the boat down the sand and into the water. The sea was calm and beautiful, hardly a wave in sight.

George jumped in and began to row out towards the island. The water lapped gently round the sides of the little boat as it cut through the waves. Timothy stood up and barked fiercely at the slap-slap of the water against the sides of the boat. If a sudden large wave came he hoped his fierce barking would scare it away.

There was a reef of very dangerous rocks surrounding Kirrin Island but George knew the safe way through them like the back of her hand.

'Almost there, Tim,' panted the little girl ten minutes later as she guided the boat carefully in-between two sharp-looking rocks. She rowed towards a natural little harbour running up to a stretch of smooth golden sand, gave one last heave on the oars and slid the boat into the inlet, its bow crunching on the sand. They had landed!

Timothy jumped out as George shipped the oars. She leaped out after him and pulled the boat high up on the beach out of reach of the tide.

Timothy looked around. He could hardly believe his eyes. There were rabbits everywhere. More rabbits than he had ever dreamed about. Hundreds of them: little ones, big ones, baby ones, old ones! He gave a very excited bark but none of them took any notice at all.

'Now, Timmy,' warned George, heaving the rucksack out of the boat. 'You're NOT to chase the rabbits, do you understand?'

Timothy was quivering from head to foot. He looked at George. Did she really mean it? She had said they were going to have an exciting time. Exciting times meant chasing rabbits, surely?

But, yes, it was clear his mistress did mean what she said. George was staring down at him looking very stern indeed. She had the kind of look on her face that meant he simply had to do as he was told.

'They're *my* rabbits and I love them all and I won't have them frightened,' she said firmly. 'And you're not to chase the seagulls either.'

'Wuff,' said Timothy, sounding very disappointed. He looked up sadly at the gulls in the sky above his head. If he could not chase rabbits or seagulls what was there to do on George's island?

'Sorry, Timmy, darling,' said George, bending down and giving him a hug when she saw his disappointed face. 'Come on, let's explore before we have our picnic.'

Rabbits scattered in all directions as Timothy scampered on ahead. He tried not to take any notice at all of the dozens of bobbing white tails as the little creatures disappeared into holes in all sorts of places: in grassy banks, under big stones, under the roots of bushes. Their homes were everywhere.

'This way, Timmy,' called George. 'Let's go into the castle.'

Soon they were having a fine time, running up the grassy bank and along the top into one of the ruined towers. Timothy gazed upwards. This was a strange building where you could see the sky through a huge hole in the roof. He ran round and round, barking excitedly.

'This tower's very tumbledown,' said George, following him in. 'But the other one is still in one piece.'

A flock of jackdaws gave out loud cries at the funny, furry brown animal they had not seen on their island before. Chack! Chack!

What are *you* doing here?

'These steps lead down to the courtyard in the middle,' explained George to Timothy, who stood under a stone archway at the top of a crooked and broken stone stairway. She ran down the steps two at a time with the puppy at her heels.

'Look, Tim, here's the mysterious room,' said the little girl. 'Go and explore!'

Timothy ran in front and found himself in a dark, stone room with an ancient fireplace set into one of the walls. He barked loudly and the sound echoed round and round and came back at him. Was there another dog living here with a voice that sounded like his? He barked again just in case there was and it needed scaring away.

'Oh, you are funny, Timmy, darling,' laughed George, giving him a hug when she saw he looked rather puzzled. 'It's only your own echo.'

'Wuff! Wuff!' barked Timothy again. Now he knew he was the only dog there he was not puzzled one little bit.

'Come on,' said George with a sudden shiver. 'It's dark and damp in here. The only light comes from those two slit windows above our heads. Let's go out into the sunshine and have our picnic, shall we?'

'Wuff,' agreed the puppy. 'Picnic' was one of his favourite words.

So the little girl and her dog sat in the centre courtyard of the mysterious castle to eat their delicious picnic. She took the food out of her rucksack and laid it out. One of the enormous stones that had fallen from the ruined tower made a very good table.

The sun was warm on the back of her neck as she ate. First the tomato sandwiches, then the homemade cake and biscuits. It all got washed down with mouthfuls of homemade ginger beer. The ginger beer tasted glorious swigged straight from the bottle.

Timothy lay in a pool of shade and chewed away on his biscuits. Joanna had put one of his special bones in the rucksack too. He gnawed away, enjoying every morsel. Then he lapped at the fresh water George had poured out from a bottle into a special picnic dog bowl her mother had bought at the pet shop in the village.

By the time they had both finished they were very full up.

George stretched out and lay with her face up to the sun. 'Mmm, Timmy, it's so gorgeous here, I feel very sleepy. Do you?'

'Wurf,' said Timothy. He *did* feel rather tired. He lay down with his nose between his paws and dozed off.

George felt her eyelids grow heavy and she dozed off too. She felt full of happiness and picnic on her island on this lovely summer day. Bees buzzed in the flowers around her and the rabbits came out to play. George and Timothy were having the best time ever!

6

A mystery

Half an hour later George woke up. The first thing she saw when she came to was a pair of dark eyes staring at her. A baby rabbit had come close to look at this human being fast asleep outside his home. The rabbit fled as George sat up, its white tail bobbing a warning to all the others.

George yawned and stretched. 'Come on, Timmy,' she said, getting up. 'I'll show you the rest of the island, then we'll play hide-and-seek or something, shall we?'

'Wurf,' said Timothy, getting up and stretching and shaking himself. 'Wurf, wurf.'

He ran on back down to the beach and George followed. 'This way,' she called. 'Round to the other side.'

They scrambled round the rocks and along the edge of the sea to the other side of the island.

'There's not much round here, only . . .' began George. Then she stopped suddenly and drew in her breath. Something rather strange and puzzling in the sand had caught her eye.

She crouched down, her heart thudding. 'Look, Timmy,' she exclaimed. 'Footprints!' A line of footprints led away from behind a rock, up to the grassy bank behind the castle.

George's frown grew even deeper and angrier. *Someone* had been trespassing on Kirrin Island. Then she remembered what she had seen from her bedroom window earlier that morning.

'I bet that's what scared those gulls this morning,' she exclaimed. 'It was someone here. What a cheek!' she cried angrily and stood up to take a good look around. 'We'd better find them and tell them to get off at once, Timmy! How dare anyone come to *our* island!'

Then, to her dismay, George suddenly heard voices and two men came into view, walking along the beach towards them. They looked strong and rough and she felt a sudden pang of fear.

'Quick, Timmy. Hide!' she hissed, her heart beating like a drum. The men had stopped and were standing at the back of the ruined jackdaw tower. They were talking in rather loud voices, completely unaware that anyone was listening.

George grabbed the puppy's collar and crawled behind a rock. She lay flat on her stomach and pulled Timothy down with her.

A low growl came from Timothy's throat. He had spotted the men too and they looked dark and dangerous to his puppy eyes.

He knew he had to protect his little mistress from any danger.

George put her hand over his muzzle. 'Ssh, Timmy,' she hissed. 'Don't make a sound. They look horrid men to me and I think it's probably better if they don't know we're here.'

The men's voices floated towards her.

'Right, Mick,' said the taller of the two. 'You reckon you can get through those rocks in the dark?'

'Piece of cake,' said the other, shorter, man in a gruff, dark voice. 'We'll bring the stuff and leave it here until the fuss has died down.'

'Right,' answered the tall man, looking around. 'No-one ever comes here by the looks of it, Jake, and the old castle is a good place to hide stuff.'

'It's on for tonight then, eh?' said Mick.

'Yeah,' Jake said with a broad grin that showed broken and stained front teeth. 'Don't forget. It's the house with the blue front door down that narrow lane behind the church.'

'Right,' said Mick with a low chuckle. 'No-one's ever going to think of looking here. Good idea of yours, Jake.'

The two men strode off round the tower and down towards the beach.

'How on earth did they get here?' whispered George. 'I didn't see a boat, did you, Timmy?'

Timothy whined softly as if to say all he had seen were rabbits and seabirds.

The flock of jackdaws that had been strutting around the castle banks flew up suddenly, filling the air with their harsh chack, chacks of alarm.

Suddenly Timothy could not resist barking any longer. The two horrid men were leaving and he had not even tried to grab their trouser-legs!

But what came out was more like a squeak than a bark as George still had her hand over his muzzle.

'Ssh!' she hissed fiercely. 'Don't make a sound.'

But the men had heard something and looked round suspiciously.

'Did you hear that, Jake?' said Mick, frowning darkly.

'What?' asked Jake.

'I don't know,' said the other man, shrugging. 'One of those wretched seagulls I expect. They make such a horrible din.'

But then Timothy really went mad. He simply could not help it. He struggled free and jumped out from their hiding place and raced round the rocks. He bounded over to the men and sank his teeth into the hem of Jake's trouser-leg. He growled and shook it as if it was a rat.

'Hey! Get off, you mutt!' shouted the burly man, kicking out at

Timothy, but the brave little dog would not let go. He dodged the big clumsy foot and grasped the material again in his sharp little teeth, pulling and pulling until the material began to tear.

The next time though, Jake's hefty toe caught the puppy unawares. George gasped with horror as a well aimed kick landed on Timothy's ribs, bowling him over and over.

'Hey!' she yelled, leaping from her hiding place. 'You leave my dog alone, you horrible man!'

She tried to run to where Timothy lay winded but Jake grabbed her and held her fast.

'What are you doing here, son?' asked the man, pinning her arms to her sides.

George struggled and tried to kick his legs. 'Let me go!' she gasped. 'This is *my* island and *you're* trespassing!'

'Your island?' scoffed Mick. 'A boy like you? More likely *you're* trespassing.'

'No, I'm *not*,' panted George, gritting her teeth and struggling even more. 'Let me go at once, do you hear?'

'How long have you been hiding?' asked Jake suspiciously. 'Did you hear us talking?'

'Mind your own business,' panted George, red in the face from her struggles. 'If you've hurt my puppy I'll tell the police and you'll be arrested for cruelty to animals.'

Jake laughed – a big, booming laugh that echoed round the old castle towers in a most sinister way. 'You're not going to tell anyone anything,' he said. 'Tie him up, Mick, and I'll deal with the scruffy mutt. We'll teach them to listen in on other people's conversations!'

'No,' yelled George as Mick took some very thick, strong string from his pocket and bound her hands together behind her back.

'Put him inside the tower,' said Jake, getting another piece of string and tying it to Timothy's collar. He pulled until Timothy stood up, then began leading him away. Timothy dug his back claws into the ground but the man simply heaved and heaved until the puppy had to follow.

'Where are you taking him?' shouted George, struggling desperately.

'Mind your own business,' laughed Mick as he dragged and pushed George round to the front of the castle. He pulled her through the archway, down the steps and across the yard, into the gloom of the dark, stone-walled, stone-roofed room inside the tower.

The strong man sat George down by the old stone fireplace with her back against the damp wall. 'Bye, kid,' he said, still grinning. 'Mind the ghosts don't get you!'

'Bring my dog back!' yelled George but it was all in vain. The two men had taken Timothy and left George alone. She struggled and struggled until the skin of her wrists and ankles were red and sore but still she couldn't get free.

At last she managed to struggle to her feet and hop over to the doorway. 'Timmy!' she yelled. 'Timmy!'

In the distance there came the sound of a boat's engine and a silver and white cruiser nosed its way out from a hidden inlet on the far side of the island. There was a flash of light as the sun caught the glass windscreen. Once it was clear of the rocks the engine roared louder and the cruiser sped away in a wash of white spray. Then there was silence.

The men had gone, taking Timothy with them. George might never see her puppy again!

7

Timothy is brave and clever

George sank to the ground with a horrible feeling of desperation inside her. She hardly ever cried. Only silly, babyish girls cried. But now she couldn't help two big salty tears sliding down her cheeks. What had promised to be an exciting and wonderful day had turned out to be the very worst day of her life!

George racked her brains for a way to escape. Her penknife was in her pocket but no matter how she twisted and turned she couldn't reach it.

It was cold in the stone room. The ground was damp and she began to feel stiff and sore. There was nothing for it but to wait until she was rescued. Joanna and her mother knew where she had gone and would soon come to look for her when it began to get dark.

If only I knew where they had taken Timmy, the little girl thought miserably. He could be miles away by now. Another tear rolled down her cheek. What shall I do without him?

She had been sitting there for a while when suddenly there came a strange noise. A shuffling, scraping sound. George's heart began to pound painfully in her chest. Had those horrible men returned? Or were there rats inhabiting the castle ruins? She loved wild animals but was not really sure she wanted rats for company!

She shuddered. George was a very brave little girl but now her courage began to fail. She remembered what Jake had said about ghosts and looked up at the dark stone roof. The corners were shadowed and mysterious. Maybe that horrible man was right and there *were* ghosts haunting Kirrin Castle.

Suddenly she heard the sound of scampering footsteps and a little black nose appeared round the stone doorway.

George gave a gasp of surprise when the nose was soon followed by a shaggy brown head with big melting eyes. Her heart gave a skip of joy.

'Timmy!' she cried. 'Timmy! You're here. I thought they'd taken you with them!'

Timothy ran over to George, wagging his tail nineteen-to-the dozen. He was so pleased to see his mistress that he jumped on to her lap and covered her face with wet, slobbery licks.

'Oh, Timmy, you're all right!' laughed George joyfully. 'Where have you been?'

George saw a long piece of string dangling from the puppy's collar. It was ragged and chewed at the end.

'Timmy! You've been tied up and have spent all this time chewing through the string. Oh, you're the cleverest dog in the whole wide world!' cried the little girl. '*And* the bravest.'

'Wuff,' barked Timothy happily. 'Wuff, wuff.'

Then George had a bright idea. If Timothy could chew through string, maybe he could chew through her bonds too.

'Now,' she said, twisting round. 'Here! Chew through this string, Timmy. Good boy! Good boy!'

The puppy knew exactly what his little mistress wanted him to do. He tore and worried at the string until that too came loose. George was free at last.

'Well done,' she cried, giving Timothy a big hug, then rubbing her sore wrists. 'Now, I'll undo my legs and we can get going.'

Soon she was on her feet, soothing her sore ankles where the string had chafed her skin. She looked very grimy and dirty with mud-streaked legs and arms and her clothes damp and stained. 'Right,' she said. 'We'd better get back to Kirrin Cottage quickly and raise the alarm. It sounded as if those men are planning a robbery and we'd better get Mummy or Father to ring the police!'

Out of the castle they ran, as fast as their legs could carry them. The tower jackdaws squawked and chatted amongst themselves as George and Timothy dashed down to the sandy inlet where their boat was moored. George gave a sigh of relief as she saw it still sat safely above the water-line.

'I was scared those horrid men had spotted it and sunk it,' she said to Timothy. 'If they had then we would have simply had to wait until we were rescued.'

George flung the empty rucksack into the boat. 'We must get back now as quickly as we can!' She pushed the dinghy down to the water's edge and jumped in. Timothy bounded ahead. One flying leap and he was in the boat. He stood in the bow waving his tail like a banner. 'Wuff,' he barked as if to say, *Hurry, George, there's no time to waste!*

'You know that flash of light we saw?' panted George, rowing as hard as she was able towards the shore. 'Well, it was the sun reflecting off the windscreen of their boat.'

'Wurf,' said Timothy from the bow.

'They must have had it hidden round the other side of the island,' said George. 'It's a wonder we didn't spot it, though.'

'Wuff,' repeated the puppy. What *he* wanted to do was see those men again. This time he would bite more than just their trouser-legs!

George rowed carefully through the dangerous rocks. She heard the lap of the sea against the sides of the boat. As long as she could hear that, she knew they were safe. It was the scrape of rocks against the hull that meant danger. It didn't do to hurry *too* much.

The robbers' plan whirled round and round in the little girl's head. *A good place to hide the stuff. No-one ever comes here. The house with the blue front door*. What a lot of exciting things she had to tell her parents when she got home!

By now, a breeze had sprung up and the sea was quite choppy. George had to struggle hard to keep the boat heading in the direction of the shore. Timothy sniffed the air. There were so many exciting things to smell when you were on the water. Salty, fishy smells and seaweedy smells and all sorts of things.

'Right,' panted George, jumping out and heaving the boat up on the sand when at last they were safely back in Kirrin Bay. 'Come on, Tim. Let's tell Mummy what's happened as soon as we possibly can!'

The two ran as fast as their legs would carry them. Across the sand they went, up the path that led to Kirrin Cottage. They had some very exciting news to tell everyone. News that simply couldn't wait!

When they arrived at the cottage, the house was completely silent. 'Mummy,' called George at the top of her voice as they hurtled through the back door. 'Mummy? Where are you?'

The kitchen was empty so they dashed through to the lounge but George's mother was nowhere to be found.

'Blow!' said George, frowning and biting her lip. 'Where *can* she have got to?'

She dashed upstairs but her mother was not up there either. Neither was Joanna. They had both disappeared.

'Blow! Blow! Blow!' exclaimed George under her breath. 'They've both gone out, Timmy. I'll just have to tell Father.' She knew her father hated being disturbed when he was working but there was nothing else for it.

'Wurf,' agreed Timothy, wagging his tail uncertainly. There had been times when they had disturbed George's father before and he knew the tall man would not be very pleased.

Down the stairs they raced and both skidded to a halt outside Father's study. Heart pounding, George knocked firmly on the door.

'Go away,' boomed a stern voice from inside. 'I'm busy with an experiment.'

'Father, it's George,' called the little girl anxiously. 'I've got something very important and exciting to tell you!'

The study door flew open. Father stood there looking very angry. 'George, you are a pest! Now go away at once!' he stormed.

'But, Father,' argued George, 'Timothy and I have just . . .'

'Whatever it is, go and tell your mother,' insisted Father. 'And *don't* disturb me again. If this experiment goes wrong I won't be able to sell the formula and there will be no money for anything. Now go away!' He went back inside and slammed the door.

George stamped her foot angrily. Why did grown-ups never take children seriously?

Timothy gave a little whine. He jumped up and licked his

mistress's hand. He hated it when people didn't listen to her. He knew it upset her very much.

'Oh, well,' sighed George, hugging the puppy, then turning back towards the kitchen. 'We'll have to find Mummy, that's all. She can't be far away.'

They searched all over the house and garden but George's mother was nowhere to be found. George could not think *where* she might be. And where was Holly? She was supposed to be coming to play at Kirrin Cottage but there was no sign of her.

Then, at the last minute, George found a note from Joanna on the kitchen table. She had been in too much of a hurry to spot it before.

'*Gone shopping*,' the note said. '*Your mother has gone to Mrs Barratt's house. She sent a message to say Holly had a headache and she would be staying at home with her instead of helping her husband out in his new shop. Your mother has gone to their house instead*.'

'Oh, blow!' exclaimed George again when she had read it. '*Now* what are we going to do?'

8

A rush to the village

'Wuff,' said Timothy, lying down and putting his head between his paws while George paced up and down wondering what to do next. It had been a very thrilling day and he was feeling rather tired.

'You're not to go to sleep,' said George firmly. 'We've *got* to tell someone about those men. Someone's going to get robbed and we've got to stop them!'

'Wurf,' said Timothy rather sleepily.

'Come on, Timmy, darling,' urged George, fetching his lead and putting it into the pocket of her jeans. 'Let's go to the village and find out where Mrs Barratt and Holly live. We'll find Mummy there and tell her what's happened.'

Timothy got to his feet. He *was* sleepy but if George wanted to take him for another walk then it was perfectly all right with him. There would be plenty of time later for a snooze.

It was quite a long walk to the village from Kirrin Cottage, through the garden and out on to the moorland path in the opposite direction from the shore.

When they reached the village, they had to pass the little harbour flanked by white painted fishermen's cottages. There was a fleet of fishing boats moored there. One or two of the fishermen waved to George and the puppy as they passed by. George had lived in Kirrin all her life and the local people knew her very well.

A special friend of George's, a fisherman's son named Alf, was mending nets beside his father's boat.

'Hello, Alf!' called George, waving her hand.

'Hello, George,' Alf replied. 'How's that puppy of yours?'

'Wuff,' barked Timothy as if to say, *I'm very well, thank you*.

George had an idea. Alf knew lots of people in the village. Maybe *he* would know where Mummy's friend lived.

She jumped off the low harbour wall and ran across the shingle to ask him.

'Never heard of anyone with that name,' said Alf, shaking his head and bending down to make a fuss of Timothy.

'She's got a little girl called Holly,' added George hopefully. 'She's a bit of a baby. Oh . . .' she continued, 'and she's got an antique husband.'

'Antique?' laughed Alf. 'Do you mean he's very old?'

'No, silly,' giggled George. 'I mean he *sells* antiques.'

'Sorry,' said Alf, shaking his head again. 'Why don't you ask Mrs Wood at the post-office stores. She knows everyone.'

'Good idea,' said George, hurrying away. 'Thanks, Alf!'

She ran back up the beach and hopped on to the wall. She took Timmy's lead from her pocket and clipped it to his collar. The little dog was not used to traffic and might run into the road. 'Come on, Timmy!'

The post-office stores in Kirrin High Street sold everything from tinned tomatoes to tintacks. The doorbell clanged as George and Timothy hurtled through.

The postmistress, Mrs Wood, was sitting on her high stool behind the counter. Her parrot, Polly, was in a cage hung high above her head.

'Wuff, wuff,' said Timothy, staring up at the cage.

'Good morning,' squawked Polly. 'Pretty morning.'

George ran across to the counter. 'Hello, Mrs Wood,' she panted. 'Do you know a lady called Mrs Barratt with a little girl named Holly? My mother's with them and I've got something frightfully important to tell her.'

'Mrs Barratt?' replied the postmistress, looking thoughtful. 'Lives in Kirrin, does she?'

'Yes,' said George rather impatiently. 'She's just moved here.'

'Oh, that will be the family in the house in Church Lane,' said

Mrs Wood.

'Which house?' asked George anxiously.

'It's called Bay House,' said Mrs Wood. 'It's the third one along. You can't miss it.'

'Oh thanks, Mrs Wood,' said George. 'Come on, Timmy!'

Timothy gave up staring at the bottom of the parrot's cage. He could never understand quite where the strange voice was coming from.

'Pretty good!' squawked Polly as the puppy scampered out with his mistress.

Down the High Street they went, past the church, then along the lane that ran beside it. There were two or three houses along there. Soon they reached Bay House. The house was painted white and had tall columns beside the front door. The door was wide open. A tall, smartly dressed man was just coming out with a briefcase in his hand. He looked surprised to see a scruffy, rather dirty child and a puppy running up the front path towards him.

'I'm George,' said George without further ado. 'I'd like to see my mother, please. She's here, I believe.'

'George?' said the man, looking puzzled. 'I'm sorry but my wife's friend has a daughter. Perhaps you've come to the wrong house.'

'No,' said George impatiently, too anxious to feel pleased she had been mistaken for a boy. '*I'm* her daughter. May I see her, please, it's frightfully important?'

The man went on looking puzzled. 'I'm just off to a meeting but they're in the back garden if you'd like to go through.' He stared at George's dirty clothes and grubby arms and legs. 'Perhaps you'd better go round the outside,' he said as an afterthought.

Inside the house, George could see some very expensive-looking antiques in the hallway. The man was probably afraid they would knock something over if they rushed through.

'Right, thanks,' called George. She unclipped Timothy's lead and he scampered on ahead. He could hear George's mother's voice and knew she would be pleased to see him.

Round the path George ran. 'Wait for me, Timmy!' she called, running to try to catch up with him. Her mother and Mrs Barratt were sitting at a little wooden table on the lawn, drinking tea out of dainty porcelain cups. The garden was full of sweet-smelling roses and shrubs. There was a big shed close to the house where Mr Barratt stored the antiques to put in his new shop. The heavy wooden door had a huge padlock across the front.

The two women looked up in amazement when Timothy appeared.

'Timmy!' exclaimed George's mother, looking quite shocked. 'What on earth are you doing here? Where's George?'

'Wuff,' said Timothy excitedly, jumping up at her. He could

smell homemade cake and his mouth watered. It seemed ages since their picnic on the island and he was very hungry indeed.

'I'm here, Mummy,' said George, appearing round the corner of the house. 'We've had a very exciting adventure this morning and I . . .'

But she didn't get any further. Her mother stood up rapidly, looking very embarrassed at the appearance of her untidy-looking child. 'George!' she cried. 'You look terrible. What have you been doing?'

'I told you, I . . .' began George but again her mother interrupted.

'I'm very sorry, Helen,' she said to her friend. 'I'll take this dirty girl home at once and give her a bath. Really, George!' she hissed in her daughter's ear. 'Did you *have* to turn up here looking like such a scarecrow?'

'But, Mummy!' protested George angrily as her mother took her arm and led her firmly round to the front of the house. Timothy scurried after them, his tail down and looking rather sheepish. It wasn't very often George's mother became angry but this time he could tell she was very annoyed indeed.

'I'm sorry,' George's mother called over her shoulder to Mrs Barratt. 'Thanks for the lovely tea.'

Down the garden path George was bundled. Out into the lane. She turned hastily to make sure Timothy was coming too. As she did so, she noticed a pale face staring out from one of the upstairs windows. It was Holly, watching her being led away. George pulled a face and stuck her tongue out rudely. How dare that horrid girl spy on her! Especially when she was getting into trouble!

9

A visit from Holly

George sulked all the way home.

Timothy walked beside her mother, his tail forlornly between his legs. He couldn't understand why his small mistress was in trouble. After all, it was quite usual to get dirty when you had been tied up by villains!

'Now go up and have a bath and change your clothes,' said George's mother when they were back home. 'It really was too bad of you to turn up looking like a ragamuffin, George. Why can't you keep clean like other little girls?'

'Because I'm *not* other little girls,' said George, scowling fiercely. She was in much too much of a huff to tell her mother about their adventure now. She stormed upstairs to the bathroom. Timothy scrambled up after her. He sat on her bed waiting for her to come out again.

'I'm not *ever* going to tell anyone now!' declared George when she returned from the bathroom looking a good deal cleaner. 'If a house gets robbed then it's not *our* fault, is it, Timmy, darling?' she added, sitting next to her puppy on the bed and putting her arm around him. She always felt better about things when she could hug him.

'Wuff,' said Timothy softly. He didn't really care about the robbers. Anything that made George unhappy, made him unhappy too.

George sat on her bed for quite a long spell. She was still sulking and feeling in a great huff when there came a knock at the front door.

Then she heard voices downstairs.

'Oh, that *is* kind of you,' said her mother to someone. 'I'm afraid George is in her bedroom sulking.'

'Sulking?' exclaimed George indignantly. 'We're not sulking, are we, Timmy?' She went to the top of the stairs to see who was there. 'We're just upset because no-one will listen to us and because Mummy doesn't understand that people can't help getting dirty sometimes.'

Timothy gave a little whine of agreement. He didn't mind getting dirty one little bit.

'Oh, blow!' said George as she peeped through the banisters and saw who was downstairs. It was Holly and she was standing at the front door talking to George's mother. 'It's that *girl*! What's *she* doing here?'

'I brought Timmy's lead back,' she heard Holly say.

'Oh, that *is* kind of you, dear,' said George's mother.

'Wuff,' said Timothy, peering through the banisters too. He really could not think how Holly came to be carrying his lead.

'I must have dropped it when Mummy dragged me away,' whispered George in his shaggy ear.

'Would you like me to take it up to her?' Holly was asking.

'If you wish,' said George's mother, stepping back so Holly could come inside. 'But I'm not sure she'll speak to you. She can be rather fierce at times, you know.'

'Yes, I know,' said Holly. 'Which is her room?'

'The little one under the eaves of the house,' said George's mother.

'Oh, blow, she's coming up!' hissed George, diving back into her room and closing the door firmly. She sat on her bed, swinging her legs to and fro and scowling like mad.

A minute later there was a timid knock.

'Hello, George. It's Holly, I've brought Timmy's lead back,' came a little voice.

George frowned and bit her lip. Maybe if they were very quiet then the horrid girl would think they had slipped out without

Mummy knowing. She felt very angry. How dare she allow that girl to come up to her room. This day was getting worse and worse.

The knock came again. This was too much for Timothy. He simply couldn't help giving a little bark. Usually when people knocked at the door he was *expected* to bark to warn the family someone was there. So why could he not do it now?

'Wuff, wuff,' said the puppy before George had a chance to stop him.

'Oh, Tim!' exclaimed George. 'You've given the game away.'

'Wuff,' said Timothy again, giving George a puzzled stare.

George thought she had better open the door before her mother realized what was going on and became annoyed again.

She walked slowly across the room and opened the door. Holly was standing there holding out the lead. 'I've brought this,' she said. 'You dropped it.'

'Thanks,' said George gruffly, taking it from her. She looked down and shuffled her feet. She supposed it was quite nice of the girl to return it.

Holly took a step back looking scared as Timothy came out to say hello. His tail wagged even though he knew the little girl was frightened of him. He couldn't give up trying to make friends, though.

'Stay!' commanded his mistress. She thought it would simply be too horrid of her to let Timothy frighten Holly when she had been kind enough to bring back his lead.

Timothy sat by her feet and stared at the little girl with long hair. Sometimes he could not understand humans at all!

'I saw you from the window,' said Holly to George, keeping a wary eye on the puppy.

'Yes,' mumbled George. 'I saw you spying on me.'

'I wasn't spying,' said Holly indignantly. 'I just wondered what was going on.' She gave a little giggle. 'You looked awfully funny. Especially when you stuck your tongue out.'

'It was *not* funny,' said George, still scowling. 'How would you like to be shown up by your mother?'

'My mother shows me up all the time,' said Holly. 'She makes me wear horrible dresses and white socks and vile shoes. At least your mother lets you wear what you like.'

'That's true,' agreed George, looking up at Holly. The little girl was still smiling. Her pale blue eyes were sparkling with mischief.

All of a sudden George couldn't help smiling too. Holly really wasn't so bad after all. She supposed it wasn't *her* fault that her mother made her wear silly dresses. Mothers could be very tiresome at times.

'I suppose I did look funny,' she admitted, the scowl disappearing and a grin taking its place. She suddenly felt a bit sorry for Holly. She would absolutely detest having to wear girls' clothes and only do girls' things the whole time.

'How *did* you get so dirty?' asked Holly curiously.

'We had an adventure,' said George. 'I was dying to tell Mummy so I just ran to your house without bothering to get washed first.' She scowled again. 'Anyway I hate washing. Boys don't wash half as much as girls.'

But Holly was more interested in what had happened to George than whether she liked washing or not. 'An adventure?' she exclaimed eagerly. 'What kind of adventure?'

And so suddenly George found herself telling Holly everything. Holly listened with her eyes as round as saucers. She kept butting in while George was telling the story.

'Is it *really* your island?' she exclaimed. 'How thrilling. I wish I had an island.'

'Well, it's actually not mine *yet*,' said George. 'But Mummy has promised to give it to me one day.' She took Holly across to her little window that overlooked the sea. From there, Holly could see the island and the castle standing proud and steadfast guarding the entrance to Kirrin Bay.

'How super,' sighed Holly. '*And* you've got a boat. I'm not allowed to have anything like that. Mummy and Daddy are too scared something dangerous will happen to me. I'm an only child you see.'

'So am I,' said George scornfully. 'But I've got Timmy and we love having adventures. We don't need human friends at all.'

'Oh, I see,' said Holly, still eyeing the puppy warily. 'Tell me more about those horrid men you saw.'

Her eyes grew rounder and rounder as George told her how she heard the men planning a robbery.

'Here, in Kirrin?' asked Holly.

'Yes,' said George. 'But then they spotted me and didn't talk about it any more.'

'No *wonder* you got so dirty,' exclaimed Holly when she heard how George had been tied up in the stone room, then rescued by the brave Timothy.

'Yes,' said George. 'But I don't really care about that. What I care about is that those men are going to steal some things from a house with a blue front door and I wanted to try to stop them.'

'A blue front door!' exclaimed Holly. '*Our* house has got a blue front door!'

George stared at the little girl in horror. 'I didn't see your front door because it was open and your father was just coming out.'

'Well, it's blue,' declared Holly. 'A deep, dark blue.'

'And they said it was down the lane behind the church!' exclaimed George in a horrified voice. 'It must be your house they're planning to rob! What on earth shall we do?'

10

Hurrying back again

Holly was looking very shocked and frightened. 'We must tell Daddy as quickly as we can!' she cried.

George's mother was nowhere in sight as the two little girls came rushing out of George's bedroom and down the stairs.

'Come on, Holly! There's no time to lose,' called George impatiently, leaping down two steps at a time. 'Where's Mummy?' she demanded of Joanna as they hurtled into the kitchen with Timothy at their heels.

'She's talking to your father in his study,' said Joanna, bustling round preparing the evening meal. 'She said they weren't to be disturbed.'

'Will you tell her I've gone to Holly's house,' panted George. 'We've got something very important to tell her father.'

'Surely you're not going before you've had your tea?' said Joanna, looking surprised. George hardly ever went anywhere unless she had eaten first.

George hesitated. She *did* feel hungry and there *was* a delicious smell of homemade ham and egg pie coming from the pantry.

'Do you want some tea before we go?' she asked Holly.

'I *would* like some but we really should hurry,' said Holly, shaking her head.

'Could you wrap me up some of that pie, please, Joanna?' said George. 'I'll eat it as we go along. Would you like some too, Holly?'

'I'm not allowed to eat while I'm moving about,' said Holly, gazing longingly at the pie as Joanna brought it out from the pantry.

'Why not?' asked George.

'Because it gives you indigestion,' said Joanna, cutting off a huge slice and wrapping it up in greaseproof paper.

'No it doesn't,' argued George. 'I've eaten food on the move millions of times and I've never had in . . . in . . .'

'Indigestion,' said Joanna with a smile.

'Go on, Holly,' urged George. 'Your mother won't know.'

'Oh, all right,' said Holly. 'The pie looks so scrumptious I don't really mind if she does. It'll be worth a telling off!'

'It'll be getting dark soon,' said Joanna, cutting a piece of pie for Holly and a very small piece to give to Timothy. 'So don't be away too long.'

'We won't,' promised George.

'And don't get indigestion!' called the kindly housekeeper as the two little girls hurried off. She chuckled to herself. It was awfully nice to see George with a human friend for a change.

'I'm not sure we can take Timmy,' said Holly as they ran outside with the puppy at their heels. She looked down at him warily. She had been very thankful that he hadn't jumped up at her even though he had quickly scoffed his piece of pie and was looking hopefully at hers. She might have screamed, then George would have called her a baby. 'Mummy doesn't like animals in the house,' she added. 'She says they make a lot of mess.'

George stopped in her tracks and took a large bite of pie. 'Well,

I'm not coming, then,' she said with her mouth full. 'I always take Timmy everywhere with me.'

'Perhaps we could leave him outside?' suggested Holly timidly.

'No,' said George, shaking her head. 'If it wasn't for him I'd still be tied up on the island waiting to be rescued. He's far too brave to be shut outside as if he had done something wrong.'

'All right,' said poor Holly, sighing. 'But I don't know what Mummy will say.'

'Sometimes it doesn't matter what grown-ups say,' said George, frowning. 'My father often sends Timothy outside but I always get him back. Grown-ups don't always know best, you know!'

'That's true,' said Holly with another sigh. This really was a strange and fierce little girl. She took a last bite of her delicious pie and licked her lips. Somehow it tasted even better because her mother didn't know she was eating it. She wasn't sure what indigestion was but she hoped she wouldn't get it all the same.

So back to Kirrin Village they went, two little girls and a puppy, gobbling up slices of ham and egg pie as they ran along the cliff path that led from the cottage. They hurried as fast as they could, down the slope and along by the harbour. There was no time to stop and talk to George's fisher friends. There were far more important matters on their minds.

It was a breezy evening with grey clouds scudding across the sky. There were white horses in the bay and darker clouds on the horizon.

One or two spots of rain hit George's face as she and Holly hurried along the High Street and into the lane behind the church.

'I hope Daddy's back from his meeting,' panted Holly, pushing open the gate and running down the path. 'Mummy will be very frightened indeed when she hears what we've got to say.'

'I only hope they believe us,' said George dubiously. 'Grown-ups have rather a horrid habit of not believing what children say, you know. Even if they're like me and never tell lies.'

'I know,' said Holly. 'Mummy doesn't believe I hate wearing dresses and would give anything for a pair of jeans like yours.'

Mrs Barratt was in her sewing room when the two girls and the puppy burst in. She had been making her daughter a new dress and almost dropped it in surprise when she heard two pairs of feet and four paws running into the house.

'Mummy? Where are you?' called Holly, rushing from room to room. 'Daddy? Are you home?'

Mrs Barratt came out of her room with a frown on her face. 'Holly! Why are you making all that noise?' She stopped when she saw George and Timothy standing there. 'Oh . . . er . . . Georgina? How nice to see you.'

'It's George,' said Holly before George could speak. 'And she's got something terrifically important to tell you and Daddy.'

'Important?' said Mrs Barratt, eyeing Timothy with disapproval. 'Has your mother asked you to come and apologize?'

'What for?' asked George. 'I haven't done anything wrong. I came to tell you that I heard two men planning to rob your house.'

'Rob our house?' came a deep voice from behind them. 'Who's making up stories, then?'

The voice belonged to Mr Barratt. He had just returned from his meeting and had come in and heard what George had said. George's heart sank. He'd looked surprised last time she'd seen him but now he just looked rather stern. How could she convince him she was telling the truth? She decided to take the bull by the horns.

'No-one's making up stories,' she insisted rather breathlessly, turning to face Holly's father. 'It's the truth.'

'Oh, Daddy!' cried Holly. 'I'm so pleased you're home.' She took his hand and pulled him towards the sitting-room. 'Come on, Daddy . . . Mummy, come and listen to George.'

Mrs Barratt was still frowning down at Timothy. The puppy had been sticking as close to George as he possibly could. He had heard the words 'leave him outside' and dreaded being tied up in a strange garden. He had also seen the lady frowning at him and knew he had to be on his very best behaviour.

'His name's Timothy,' said George when she saw Holly's father gazing at the puppy. 'He's quite clean and he comes everywhere with me.'

'Righty-ho,' said Mr Barratt with a smile. 'Come on, then, you'd better tell me all these exciting things before you burst.'

George grinned at Holly's father and heaved a little sigh of relief. He seemed a very nice man after all. 'Well,' she said when they were all sitting down. 'It's like this . . .'

11

A storm

George told the story of their adventure with the two rough men as quickly as she could. In fact the words tumbled out so fast that she had to go over it again.

'So they said a house with a blue front door, did they?' asked Mr Barratt with a frown. 'But there must be more than one house in Kirrin with a door that colour.'

'Yes,' said George, 'but not down a lane behind the church.'

'I see,' said Mr Barratt, nodding thoughtfully. 'And you're *sure* that's what they said?'

'Positive,' said George. 'I never make mistakes of that kind.'

'Are you *sure* you're not making all this up?' asked Mrs Barratt dubiously. She wasn't at all certain she believed what this strange little girl had been telling them. 'How would anyone know we've got anything worth stealing?'

'Of course, I'm sure,' said George angrily and rather rudely. 'I couldn't possibly make up something like that.'

Mr Barratt got out of his chair and walked up and down the room looking rather thoughtful. 'These things do get around,' he said. 'Someone could have seen me unloading antiques for my shop and storing them in the shed. *They* would certainly be worth stealing.'

'Don't you think we should phone the police?' said George urgently. 'Those men looked very determined and awfully dangerous.'

'We haven't had the phone put in yet,' said Mrs Barratt, gazing at the forthright little girl.

'Someone will have to go to the police station,' said Mr Barratt.

'Yes,' agreed George. 'PC Moon will be awfully pleased to be able to catch some burglars.'

'I'd better get down there at once,' said Mr Barratt.

'Please don't go and leave us, Harold,' implored Mrs Barratt. 'If Georgina's story is true, those men could turn up whilst you're gone.'

'George,' said George, scowling. 'My name's George.'

'Oh, very well, then,' said Mrs Barratt, shaking her head. '*George*.'

'And we can't *all* go in case they *do* come,' said Holly anxiously. 'So what are we going to do?'

'Wait until they turn up, then catch them red-handed,' said

George matter-of-factly. 'Timmy will help.'

'They might be violent,' said Mrs Barratt with a shiver. 'And Timothy is only a puppy.'

'But he's a very brave puppy,' said George indignantly.

'Yes, yes,' said Mr Barratt, still looking thoughtful. 'I think George is right, though. If we can catch them actually breaking into the shed then they won't be able to deny that they're robbers.'

'That's right,' said George excitedly. 'We can be as quiet as mice, then pounce on them. What fun!'

'We'll just have to sit it out, then,' said Mr Barratt. 'I'd like to take you home, George, but I don't want to leave my wife and Holly.'

'I don't want to go home,' said George indignantly. 'Joanna's going to tell Mummy where I am. I don't want to miss another adventure!'

So George, Timothy, Mr and Mrs Barratt and Holly waited in the front room until darkness fell. It seemed very strange and thrilling waiting for robbers to turn up. It was frightening too. George gave a little shiver of excitement. Her stomach felt rather fluttery. She was very glad indeed that Holly's father was there. She knew he wouldn't let anything bad happen to any of them.

Timothy could feel the excitement too. His ears were pricked up higher than ever. They strained for any sound that would pierce the gloom outside.

The little rain clouds that had dotted the sky when George and Holly had set off for Bay House had turned into one solid dark mass. It soon began to rain very hard, pitter, patter against the windows.

It had become windy too and George could hear the trees blowing about outside. Then there was a crack and a bolt of lightning raced across the sky.

'Oh,' said Holly, giving a little squeal. 'I hate thunderstorms.'

'They don't hurt you,' said George scornfully. 'They're great fun to watch.'

'No, thank you,' said Mrs Barratt, giving George a strange look and holding Holly's hand very tightly. She had never met a child who liked storms before.

It's a shame Mrs Barratt is frightened of so many things, thought George to herself. No wonder Holly is such a scaredy-cat.

Timothy sat very quietly close to George's feet. It was a horrid evening out there and he had the feeling that one wrong move and he would be made to go outside. The lady didn't like him and the little girl was scared of him, although he didn't know why. At least the man had smiled at him, though. Timothy comforted himself with that thought. Maybe things weren't so bad after all.

Mrs Barratt went round switching on all the lights. She drew all the curtains close together to shut out the storm. 'I prefer *not* to see the lightning,' she said, going back to sit with Holly.

'Too-whit, too-whoo,' came the sound of an owl from a nearby tree and everyone almost jumped out of their skin.

'What was that?' cried Mrs Barratt.

'It's all right,' said George with an air of someone who knew about those things. 'It's only a tawny owl.'

'Oh, dear,' said Holly, sitting so close to her mother she was almost on her lap. 'I wish this wasn't happening.'

'I don't,' said George, sounding rather braver than she felt. 'I like adventures . . . I think!' she added, suddenly feeling not at all sure that she liked this particular one! It was very strange indeed sitting in a storm waiting for robbers to turn up.

'What shall we do if they come?' asked Holly in a small voice.

'We need a plan,' said George.

'Don't you worry about a plan,' said Mr Barratt. 'If we hear them I'll run out with a stick and scare them away.'

'Oh, Harold, they might attack you,' said Mrs Barratt, sounding horrified.

'We'll all shout and make lots of noise,' said George. 'And Timmy will bark.'

'That's a good idea,' said Holly. 'Then they'll think there are lots and lots of people chasing them.'

'No,' said Mr Barratt sternly. 'I'll see to it, don't any of you worry. I don't want any of you women to be in danger.'

Women! thought George. It's bad enough being a *girl* let alone being called a *woman*!

They had sat there for almost an hour, although it seemed a good deal longer, when suddenly there was a noise outside. It was the sound of the front gate opening and someone coming down the path towards the house; two people, their footfalls echoing on the brick pathway.

Timothy gave a low growl. He did not like the sound of those heavy footsteps one little bit. He began to quiver with excitement.

If *only* George would let him bark he could frighten the people away. But her hand on his muzzle told him she wanted him to keep quiet so he sat as still as a mouse, his heart beating like a drum.

'Who is it?' whispered Holly, wriggling even closer to her mother. 'I'm frightened.'

'Don't worry,' whispered her father. 'And for goodness' sake keep quiet!'

Everyone was holding their breath. The only sound in the room was the heavy tick-tock of the antique grandfather clock in the corner. The sound seemed a hundred times louder than it really was.

'I'll peep through the curtain,' said George. 'If it's the robbers we can jump out and scare them away!'

'No . . .' began Mr Barratt as George got up and went towards the window. 'Don't . . .'

All of a sudden there was a tremendous flash of lightning and all the lights went out.

'Oh, blow!' said George in a loud voice, trying to feel her way forward. She bumped her knee painfully into the arm of a chair. 'What's happened?'

'A power cut, I expect,' said Mrs Barratt in a trembly voice. 'When we lived in London we often had power cuts during storms.'

'I don't like it, Mummy,' wailed Holly, feeling very scared indeed.

'Shut up!' hissed George, sitting back down. Although she would not admit it, she was scared too. Her heart pounded so hard in her chest that it hurt and so did her knee where she had banged it. Without any lights the robbers could easily creep round the back without being seen. One might even creep indoors! There were valuable antiques in here too.

What on earth were they going to do?

12

A plan

Suddenly there came a very loud knock at the front door. Everyone gazed at one another. Surely burglars wouldn't knock?

'Visitors,' said Mr Barratt, giving a sigh of relief. 'You stay there, you three, I'll go and see who it is.'

Mr Barratt bumped and crashed his way to the front door. George wished she had brought her torch.

The sound of voices came from the hallway. Timothy's tail began to wag and he gave a little whine when he heard them.

'Is Georgina with you?' came Father's voice.

George frowned. What on earth was he doing here?

Mrs Barratt jumped up as both George's parents came into the room. They were both wearing mackintoshes and boots. Father was holding a torch. They looked very wet indeed and Father looked very annoyed.

'I'm sorry there's no lights,' said Mr Barratt as they came

through. 'The lightning has caused a power cut.'

'Fanny!' Mrs Barratt exclaimed. 'We thought you were . . .'

'George, we wondered where you had got to,' said George's father, shining the torch on her before poor Mrs Barratt had time to finish her sentence. 'You're very naughty going off like that and staying out after dark. We were extremely concerned,' he added, frowning deeply.

'I'm sorry,' said George. 'But I had something very important to tell Mr and Mrs Barratt.'

George's mother introduced her husband to everyone.

'You should have sent her home,' said her father, sounding very annoyed indeed. His wife had dragged him out of his study to come here and he was extremely upset.

'It's all right, Quentin,' said his wife gently, putting her hand on his arm. 'George and Timmy are safe, that's the main thing. Come along, George, dear, we'll take you home now.'

'We're waiting for robbers,' said George, sitting down and folding her arms. 'And Timmy and I are going to help scare them away so I'm not coming home yet.'

'Robbers?' said Father, frowning. 'Don't be silly, George.'

'I'm not being silly,' began George, flaring up as usual. 'I heard them planning to steal Mr Barratt's antiques.'

'Wuff, wuff,' said Timothy, agreeing with his mistress.

'Is this true?' asked her father, frowning even more deeply than ever.

'Apparently,' said Mrs Barratt.

'It sounds rather far-fetched to me,' said George's father, still refusing to believe the truth.

'Now, now, Quentin,' said his wife. 'You know our daughter never tells lies. If she says she overheard someone planning a robbery then you know it to be true.'

'Yes, you're right,' said her husband, nodding. He turned to Mr Barratt. 'Have you telephoned the police?'

Mr Barratt explained that they had not yet had a phone put in.

'Then someone will have to go and tell them,' said George's father.

'Yes,' said George. 'And quickly.'

'I didn't want to leave my wife and the children on their own,' explained Mr Barratt.

'So we were just waiting,' added Holly with a shiver.

'Hmm,' said George's father, stroking his chin and looking rather thoughtful. 'Perhaps we had better all stay here until they turn up then.'

'I think it really would be better to let the police know,' said Holly in a small voice. 'We can't actually *arrest* them and if they run off they might go and rob someone else instead.' Everyone turned to look at her. Her face was pale in the beam of George's father's powerful torch.

'By Jove, she's right,' said George's father admiringly. 'Fanny and I will go down to the police station and inform them what's likely to happen. You stay here with the others, Harold.'

'Fine,' agreed Holly's father. 'Be as quick as you can.'

The room was plunged into darkness again and George's parents were gone.

'I wish you had some candles, Mummy,' wailed Holly, alarmed once more. George's parents needed their torch as the streetlights had gone out too.

'Sorry, darling,' said her mother. 'They were one of the things I hadn't got round to buying yet.'

'It's better if we sit in the dark,' said George. 'They'll think there's no-one at home.'

'That's true,' agreed Holly with another little shiver.

Outside, the storm had abated. The wind dropped and there was a deathly silence. Then, suddenly, the hairs on the back of Timothy's neck stood on end.

A deep growl came from his throat. He had heard a sound the humans could not hear: the swish of bushes as someone climbed over the back hedge and the sound of heavy boots swooshing across wet grass. Then his sharp ears caught the sound of someone picking a strong padlock with a special tool that burglars use!

The robbers had arrived!

Timothy gave the loudest and fiercest growl that he possibly could.

'What's he growling at?' asked Holly in a small, fearful voice as Timothy growled again.

'He's heard something,' whispered George, putting her hand on the puppy's neck. 'He's got the best ears in the world.'

'I'd better go and see,' said Mr Barratt, getting up.

'Timmy and I will come too,' said George.

'No, you stay here,' commanded Mr Barratt, fumbling his way out to the hall where he had a strong walking-stick.

'I'm jolly well not being left out,' said George crossly. 'If it wasn't for me and Timmy you wouldn't know anything about the robbers.'

She followed Mr Barratt out of the room.

Timothy scampered after her. He couldn't wait to get his teeth into those robbers again. He still hadn't got his revenge for being tied up on the island.

With George creeping behind, Mr Barratt slipped through to the kitchen. He peered out of the window. From there, he could see the shed where his valuable antiques were stored.

Suddenly there was a flash from a torch sweeping round inside the shed. It briefly lit up the open doorway. The padlock was hanging loose where the robbers had picked it. They were already inside stealing the goods!

Just then, the moon came out from behind a cloud and George could see two shadowy figures moving around inside the shed, filling large sacks with valuable things.

'What are we going to do?' she whispered.

'It would be stupid to tackle them,' said Mr Barratt, shaking his head. 'They look jolly big and strong to me. The best we can hope for is that the police arrive quickly.'

George was shuffling from one foot to the other impatiently. She hated hanging around for things. There absolutely *had* to be something they could do!

13

George has an idea

All at once, Timothy started to growl even louder. He could smell those horrid men who were raiding Mr Barratt's antiques. He simply couldn't stand by and let them get away with it.

'Ssh!' hissed George, putting her hand over his muzzle. 'If they hear you they'll run off.'

Inside the shed, the men *had* heard something.

'What's that?' hissed Jake, lifting his head to listen with a dark frown across his face.

'Sounded like a dog to me,' said Mick, pausing and raising his head too.

'You never said they'd got a dog,' hissed Jake.

'Never seen one,' said Mick, shaking his head. 'I've been watching the place for a week and never spotted no dog.'

'Well, it must be indoors, otherwise it would have been out here like a shot,' said Jake. 'We'd better get on with it.' He grabbed a priceless clock from the shelf and put it into his sack.

Indoors, George and Holly's father were still spying from the window.

'I wish the police would hurry,' whispered George, beginning to feel rather anxious. Surely her parents would have reached the police station by now?

'Don't worry,' Mr Barratt assured her. 'I have great faith in our policemen. They'll be here very soon, I'm sure.'

But although they waited and waited, the police didn't come. Timothy was getting very impatient, growling and pawing at the floor.

Then one of the men appeared in the doorway of the shed carrying a heavy sack over his shoulder. He looked around. 'Come on, Mick,' he hissed. 'That's enough.'

'Oh, blow! They're going,' said George. 'What shall we do?'

Jake waited but his companion didn't appear so he went back inside the shed. Suddenly George knew she had to do something.

'I'll run and lock them in,' whispered the brave little girl to Mr Barratt. 'Stay, Timmy!' she added. 'Stay here. I'll call you if I need you!'

'No, you mustn't . . . !' began Mr Barratt but George had already opened the back door and slipped out. Luckily, the moon had gone back behind a cloud and the garden was once more in darkness.

Quickly and silently the little girl tiptoed across the lawn. She was holding her breath and her heart was thumping with fright. If the men came out and discovered her she could be in very grave danger.

Inside the shed, Mick and Jake were having an argument.

'I said, that's enough!' insisted Mick. 'We've got plenty. Come on, let's go!'

They both headed for the door just as George reached it. She hurled herself against it and slammed it shut.

Mr Barratt was running behind her. He put his strong shoulder to the door while George quickly clicked the padlock closed.

'Well done, George,' panted Mr Barratt. 'Very well done!'

'Hey!' yelled one of the men. 'Let us out!' A hammering and banging came from inside.

'Ha, ha!' called George, laughing. 'Hard luck, you two! You're caught now until the police get here!'

'Come on,' said Mr Barratt. 'Let's get back inside. There's nothing more we can do.'

Timothy was waiting by the back door, shaking with excitement. How he would have loved to get his teeth into one of those men!

'They're locked in, Timmy,' said George delightedly. 'Caught for ever and ever!'

But the two robbers weren't caught for ever and ever. No sooner had George and Mr Barratt gone back inside than there came the sound of smashing glass. They had broken the shed window and were climbing out!

This was too much for Timothy. He knew exactly what was happening. The men weren't prisoners at all. They were escaping and he had to stop them!

The little dog turned and ran back outside. Barking like mad, he flung himself at the robbers just as the second one was clambering from the window.

Timothy got hold of one of the sacks in his very sharp teeth. He pulled and pulled, growling very fiercely, shaking and shaking as if it were a rat.

Then pandemonium broke loose.

'It's that same dog what was on the island!' yelled Mick, kicking out at Timothy. 'How did you escape? Get off, you mutt!'

But Timothy was wiser now. He dodged round the heavy kicks, all the time hanging on to the sack for dear life. Nothing this horrid man could do would make him let go.

The robber ran across the garden with Timothy still hanging on. Sometimes he was swung into the air but he held on for dear life and wouldn't let go.

The other man was getting away. Running across the lawn and making for the front fence.

'Quick! He's getting away!' yelled George. To her surprise Holly ran out from indoors. She had been watching from the window. She dashed across the lawn and stuck out her foot right in the robber's path. He tripped and fell heavily, landing face down in the mud. He scrambled to his feet and made off.

The sound of shrieking police sirens cut through the air as two police cars skidded to a halt by the gate. PC Moon and four other officers got out just as the robber flashed past.

'Fetch, Timmy!' yelled George but the puppy needed no

encouragement. He let go of the sack and shot off through the gate after the robber. Two policemen followed hot on his heels.

They all caught up with Jake in the churchyard. He was brought down by a flying tackle from one of the policemen.

Timothy helped by tearing a large piece out of Jake's sock and biting his ankle hard.

'Wuff,' he said, feeling very satisfied as the policeman led a sorry-looking villain back to a waiting police car. 'Wuff, wuff!'

14

The end of the adventure

Timothy picked up the ragged piece of the robber's sock and ran back to look for his mistress. He knew she would be very pleased indeed!

He found her in the garden with Holly and her parents. The robber, Mick, was being led away by one of the other officers.

Timothy laid the piece of sock triumphantly at George's feet.

'Good boy!' cried the proud little girl, bending to kiss and hug him. 'Clever boy!'

'My word, he's a brave little fellow,' said one of the officers admiringly.

'I know,' said George. 'Brave and clever, the best in the world.'

To George's surprise, Holly gave Timothy a hug too. He gave her a lick. He was surprised that this other little girl wanted to be his friend after all.

'I know he won't hurt me now,' said Holly, looking up at George.

'He can tell the difference between friends and enemies. Not like that dog that bit me when I was little.'

'What dog?' asked George, looking rather puzzled.

'A big dog,' explained Holly. 'I was only being friendly but Mummy said he thought I wanted to hurt him so he bit me.'

'What a silly dog,' said George. 'So you thought all dogs were the same?' She suddenly understood why Holly had been scared of Timothy.

'Yes,' said Holly, hugging the clever puppy again. 'But now I know better.'

'You'd better come inside and explain how you knew about this robbery,' said PC Moon, getting out his notebook. 'We've been trying to catch these men for a long time so I shall be very interested to hear your story.'

Indoors they all trooped. George's mother and father, two muddy little girls and a very dirty small dog, Mr Barratt and the burly policeman.

'Hurrah! Hurrah! They didn't get away!' sang George. 'What a thrilling time we're having.' But although she wouldn't admit it, her legs felt like jelly now the excitement was all over. She felt sure boys' legs *never* felt like jelly.

As they arrived indoors, the lights came back on.

'Oh, thank goodness!' exclaimed Mr Barratt.

'Are you all right, darlings?' Mrs Barratt exclaimed, running to hug Holly and her husband. She had watched the whole episode from the kitchen window, too frightened to help.

'Fine,' said Holly. 'Did you see Timmy? Wasn't he brave?'

'He was indeed,' said Mrs Barratt, bustling about making tea for everyone. 'You all were.'

As they sat in the front room drinking mugs of hot tea, George suddenly felt very tired. She gave a huge yawn. It had been such n exciting day.

'I think we'd better get you home, George,' said her mother. 'A hot bath and bed for you.'

'Come along,' said the policeman kindly, closing his notebook and getting up. 'I'll take you home in the police car. You can give me a statement later.'

'Thank you, George,' said Mr Barratt before they left. 'One or two of my valuable things have been broken but most are safe.'

'That's good,' said George, shaking his hand.

'And thank *you*, Timothy,' said the man, bending to pat him. 'You're just about the bravest puppy I've ever seen.'

'Wuff,' said Timothy as if to say, *You're welcome*.

'Come and play tomorrow if you like,' said George to Holly as she went down the front path with her. The little girl had been very brave during the robbery. Braver than George had ever thought she could be. They could have a super time playing together now that Holly wasn't afraid of Timothy any more.

'I'll ask Mummy,' said Holly, smiling and looking down at her muddy dress. 'Do you realize she hasn't told me off for getting dirty,' she added in a whisper.

'So she hasn't,' said George, grinning. 'After this she might even buy you a pair of jeans.'

'Hope so!' said Holly, giggling.

'Don't worry if she doesn't,' said George. 'You can always borrow a pair of mine if you feel like getting dirty!'

Holly was still grinning as they all waved goodbye.

PC Moon started the car's engine. Down the lane they went: George and Timothy, Mummy and Father safely tucked in the back. George gave a sigh. What an exciting day it had been!

At Kirrin Cottage, the policeman waited while George had a nice hot bath and changed into her pyjamas.

When Joanna heard what had happened she gave Timothy a big bone as a hero's reward. George's mother made him take it into the kitchen but for once he was quite happy for his little mistress to be in one room while he was in another.

PC Moon sat with George's parents in the sitting-room waiting for her. 'Now,' he said when she came down from her bath wrapped in her snug tartan dressing-gown. 'Perhaps you would tell me all about it, Miss.'

'George,' said George, scowling.

'Oh, sorry. George . . .' said the policeman, grinning.

So George had to tell her story all over again.

'My word,' said her father when she had finished. 'You certainly were a brave little girl. You should give yourself a pat on the back. You've probably saved Mr Barratt thousands of pounds.'

'Timmy was brave too,' said George. 'One of them might have

escaped if it hadn't been for him.'

'He was indeed,' said her father with a smile. 'And just for once, George, he can sleep upstairs in your room as a reward.'

'Can he really, Father?' said George, her blue eyes shining. 'That would be marvellous.'

'Just once, mind you,' said her father, trying to look stern but smiling instead.

'Oh, thank you!' George ran across and hugged her father very tightly.

'All right,' said her mother, smiling too. 'Bed now, George and Brave Timmy . . . both of you!'

George called Timothy and, together, they raced up the stairs to George's cosy little room tucked under the roof of the old house.

'He seems to know where to go all right,' said PC Moon, laughing as George's parents showed him out.

'Yes,' said her mother. 'He's a very clever little dog.'

In her room, George took off her dressing-gown and patted the bed. 'Come on, Timmy, darling. Your usual place.'

Timothy jumped up and turned round and round making himself a nest in the blankets. Then he lay down with a huge, puppy sigh. His eyes began to close. He really was very tired indeed.

'Well, that was an adventure and a half, wasn't it, Timmy?' said

George, crawling under the covers and putting her weary head on her soft pillow.

From outside came the hoot of an owl and the swishy music of the waves on the shore.

'I hope we have lots more adventures, don't you, Tim?' murmured George sleepily.

But Timothy did not hear what she said. He was curled up, fast asleep. He was already dreaming of lots more thrilling times to come!

ADVENTURE
FACTS
GUIDE

HOW TO TRACK A TRAIL

You are on the trail of robbers or crooks, but then you lose sight of them! To be able to choose the right route you need to know some simple tracking skills.

TIME MATTERS

1. The time of day can have an effect on what you see.
2. The evening is best for tracking, as the sun casts a shadow on footprints, making them easier to see.
3. If tracking at night make sure you stay low to the ground and use a torch to help highlight footprints.
4. There are some simple ways to tell how long ago a footprint was made:

> **Has the sun dried it out or is the print still slightly damp?**

> **Has the wind smoothed out the edges of the print?**

> **When looking for flattened, trodden-on grass, remember that it will spring back up in around 24 hours.**

FOOTPRINTS

1. Look for footprints in patches of sandy, or wet, ground. Get down low and turn your head to look at an angle.
2. Make sure you've got a tape measure, or ruler, with you. Measure the footprints as you find them. There might be lots of different tracks and if you know the size of the prints you are looking for you can be sure that you are following the right ones.
3. You should also measure the distance between each track. This will tell you how tall the person you are following is and whether they were running or walking; the longer the stride the faster the person was moving. The deeper the footprint is in the earth the heavier they are. Heavy footprints could also mean that the person you are following is carrying something big.
4. If tracking animals remember to look for, and identify, droppings. Wear disposable gloves if you are going to handle animal droppings as they might contain germs and bacteria that can make you ill.
5. Invest in a detailed animal track guide. This will make it easier to identify the different animal tracks, so you will know if you are tracking a bad-guy or a bear!

TRAIL CLUES

- Keep your eyes open for hair or fabric snagged on branches.
- Carry tweezers, clear tape and plastic bags to collect any evidence.
- A magnifying glass can be useful for looking at anything you find.
- Look out for bent or broken tree branches and tall grass that has been pushed down or walked on. These are signs that someone may have gone off the main trail.
- Keep an eye out for anything out of the ordinary such as overturned stones, mud marks on rocks and logs and broken cobwebs.

CAST AND KEEP

You will need:

> **Plaster of Paris**
> **Talcum powder**
> **Lolly sticks**

1. Use the lolly sticks to make a square around the footprint.
2. Mix the plaster following the instructions on the packet.
3. Sprinkle talcum powder on the print. This will help the plaster to stick to the print.

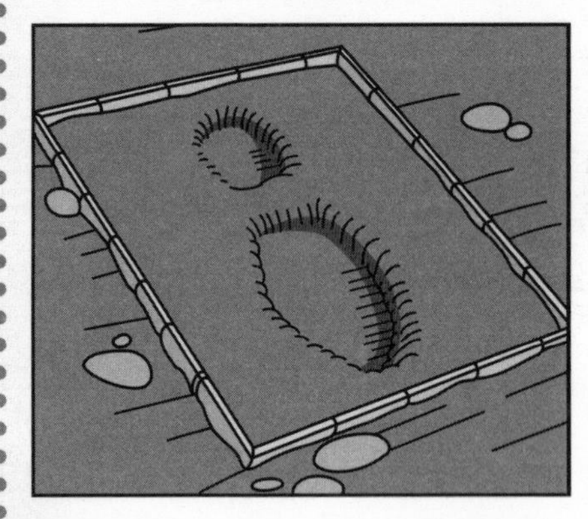

4. Pour the plaster around the outside of the print so it flows slowly into the middle. Do not pour the plaster straight on to the print, as the force of the flow would ruin it.
5. When the print is half-full with plaster, put some lolly sticks into it. This will make the cast stronger.
6. Wait for about half an hour.
7. When the cast is hard, carefully lift it out of the ground.

8. Wait for 24 hours to allow the plaster to set. Then gently clean it with a soft brush.

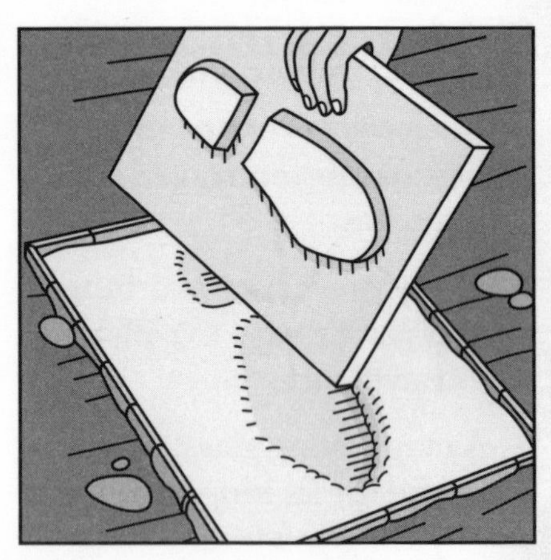

MATCH THE TRACKS

Can you match the tracks to the animals?

HERON **FOX** **SQUIRREL** **WEASEL** **DEER** **BADGER**

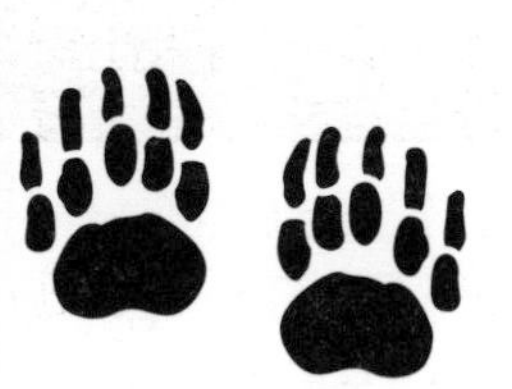

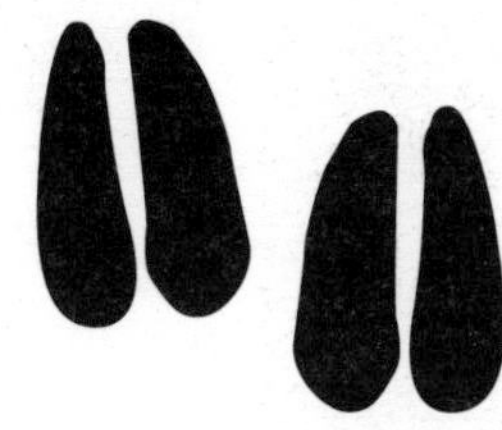

1. .... 2. .... 3. ....

4. .... 5. .... 6. ....

Answers on page 333.

Further Information

I hope that you've learned a lot about both your new puppy and how to have an adventure, but what I can tell you is just a start. If you want more information on how to care for your new dog, or tips and information from professional explorers, have a look at these websites and organizations. Soon you'll be having as much fun as Timmy and I always do!

- Places of Interest -

www.nationaltrust.org.uk
www.english-heritage.org.uk
www.nationaltrust.org.au
www.nsw.nationaltrust.org.au
www.nationaltrust.org
www.nps.gov

- Rambling/Hiking -

www.ramblingclubs.com
www.americanhiking.org

- Camping/Adventure Holidays -

www.youthinformation.com
www.oeg.net.au
www.outwardbound.net

- Nature Conservation -

www.greenpeace.org
www.nature.org
www.acfonline.org.au

- Country Code -

www.countrysideaccess.gov.uk/things_to_know
www.imba.com/about/trail_rules.html

- Caves and Cave Safety -

www.nps.gov
www.caves.org
www.caves.org.au
www.british-caving.org.uk

- Water Safety -

www.fenswaterways.com/wsk/
www.water-safety.org
www.rospa.com/leisuresafety/water

- Meteorology -

www.bom.gov.au/lam
www.srh.noaa.gov/srh/jetstream
www.bbc.co.uk/weather/weatherwise
www.metoffice.gov.uk
www.nws.noaa.gov

- Pet Care -

www.aspca.org/
www.rspca.org.uk
www.petcare.org.uk
www.hsus.org

- Fossils -

www.nhm.ac.uk/nature-online/earth/fossils/index
www.culture.gov.au/articles/fossils
www.geolsoc.org.uk

PUZZLE ANSWERS :

P224/5 SLIDER CODE - George is waiting at home : P226 RULER CODE - The gold is lost : P226/7 ROUTE CODE - Send help to the old stable now : P227 MASK - I love to solve coded messages : P228 CODED CROSSWORD - Across: 1 Hare, 2 Pig, 5 Deer, 6 Goat, 8 Dog, 9 Giraffe. Down: 1 Hedgehog, 3 Gorilla, 4 Rat, 7 Wolf : P331 MATCH THE TRACKS - 1. Badger 2. Deer 3. Squirrel 4. Heron 5. Fox 6. Weasel

PICTURE CREDITS : Imagery Copyright © 2009 artist listed below. Used under licence from Shutterstock.com

115 - Group of Dogs - Eric Isselée
116 - Dog and Cat - Michael Pettigrew
116 - Sleepy Pug - mlorenz
116 - Shaggy Dog - Eric Isselée
117 - Puppy Cuddle - Ipatov
117/118 - Bones (background) - Oculo
118 - Puppy on Cushion - iNNOCENt
118 - Puppy with Toy - Thomas Mounsey
119 - Puppy Playing- Denis Babenko
119 - Big Puppy Ears - Dr.Margorius
120 - Caveman - PhotoSky 4t com
121 - Boots - oddech
121 - Torch - Matthew Cole
121 - Helmet - Zholobov Vadim
122 - Sea Cave - Dorn1530
122 - Cave Painting - Roxana Gonzalez
123 - Bats in Cave - TheSupe87
123 - Stalactites - Douglas Knight
123 - Proteus Worm - Domen Lombergar
125 - Ultrasound - Monkey Business Images
125 - Dolphins - Robert Sprigg
126 - Hermit Crab - Nancy Kennedy
126 - Limpits On Rock - Ismael Montero Verdu
126 - Anemone - Insuratelu Gabriela Gianin
127 - Star Fish - naturediver
127 - Shark Eggs - Anke van Wyk
127 - Shells (background) - aleksm
219 - Dog in a Basket - Hannamariah
220 - Puppy Training - Crystal Kirk
220 - Puppy Running - beltsazar
221 - Pair of Dogs - MalibuBooks
221 - Naughty Boxer - Tad Denson
222 - Trilobite - Dr. Morley Read
222 - Ammonite - Ismael Montero Verdu
223 - Dinosaur Print - michael ledray
223 - Grasshopper in Amber - Roy Palmer
223/225 - Dinosaurs (background) - Ismael Montero Verdu
223/225 - Dinosaurs (background) - Andrew Chin
224 - Plateosaurus - Andreas Meyer
225 - T Rex - Vaclav Volrab
225 - Stegosaurus - Jean-Michel Girard
225 - Allosaurus - Jean-Michel Girard
228 - Ruler - LVector
327 - Foot Print - Hirlesteanu Constantin-Ciprian
328 - Animal Print - Pichugin Dmitry
329 - Sheep Wool - Anita Charlton
329 - Animal Tracks (background) - Ismael Montero Verdu
331 - Animal shapes - Goran J / Robert A Hillman / Helen Cingisiz

Read more adventures of George and Timmy
as members of The Famous Five in

Five On A Treasure Island

Five Go Adventuring Again

Five Run Away Together

Five Go To Smuggler's Top

Five Go Off In A Caravan

Five On Kirrin Island Again

Five Go Off To Camp

Five Get Into Trouble

Five Fall Into Adventure

Five On A Hike Together

Five Have A Wonderful Time

Five Go Down To The Sea

Five Go To Mystery Moor

Five Have Plenty Of Fun

Five On A Secret Trail

Five Go To Billycock Hill

Five Get Into A Fix

Five On Finniston Farm

Five Go To Demon's Rocks

Five Have A Mystery To Solve

Five Are Together Again

The Famous Five Short Story Collection

The Famous Five's Survival Guide